Advance Praise for *In Love With a Thug*

"Finally a gritty black-on-black love story. Reginald's writing is dynamic and suspenseful."

—BRENDA L. THOMAS, *Essence* Bestselling Author of *Threesome*, *Fourplay*, and *Every Woman's Got a Secret*

"WARNING: Reginald does it again! Y'all ain't ready for this! But if you are—get your popcorn and lock the door. You will not want to be disturbed."

—*Don Diva Magazine*

"I've been in love with a thug but never one like this. Reginald L. Hall has definitely put a twist on this!!"

—KASHAMBA WILLIAMS, *Essence* Bestselling Author of *Driven*

"Reg, do ya thang, dawg. The coolest gay dude I know. This book is gonna hit 'em hard. Do ya thang."

—JAHEIM, platinum recording artist of *Ghetto Love* and *Still Ghetto*

"From the Streetz to erotic gay literature. My boy has proved his point and oh hell yes, this novel has been truly stamped hood-certified."

—OMARION, triple platinum album recording artist and former B2K lead singer

"Scandalous, controversial, and captivating! A tale of passion waiting to explode."

—TU-SHONDA L. WHITAKER, *Essence* No. 1 Bestselling Author of *The Ex Factor*

"Reginald L. Hall in *In Love With a Thug* delivers a raw, no-holds-barred, roller-coaster of a ride that will leave you shaken and wobbly, but ultimately better because of the ride!"

—LEE HAYES, Author of *Passion Marks*, *A Deeper Blue: Passion Marks II* and *The Messiah*

"*In Love With a Thug* makes you look for love in all the wrong places!"

—HICKSON, publisher of *Convict's Candy*, *Ghettoheat* and *Harder*

"A sizzling, sexy novel that I personally call *Heat!*"

—AYANA KAHN, mother of the Legendary House of Kahn

Comment on *Smoking Cigarettes*

"Reginald's character portrays a similar character of Winter from the *The Coldest Winter Ever*."

—The RAWSISTAZ Reviewers

"Reginald's erotic writing brings a new voice to urban literature who can be likened to the queen Zane."

—*The Philadelphia Daily News*

Praise for *Memoir: Delaware County Prison*

"Reginald takes you inside a place that's been kept secret. It's unveiling and down right spicy (hot)."

—*Vibe* magazine

"Ladies, listen up—fellas, listen up! A tale that set the city on fire!"

—Clear Channel Radio

Strebor on the Streetz

IN
LOVE
WITH A
Thug

Reginald L. Hall

STREBOR BOOKS

NEW YORK LONDON TORONTO SYDNEY

Strebor Books
P.O. Box 6505
Largo, MD 20792
http://www.streborbooks.com

ISBN-13 978-1-59309-148-4
ISBN-10   1-59309-148-6
LCCN 2007923715

First Strebor Books trade paperback edition August 2007

Cover design: www.mariondesigns.com

10   9   8   7   6   5   4

Manufactured in the United States of America

For information regarding special discounts for bulk purchases, please contact Simon & Schuster Special Sales at 1-800-456-6798 or business@simonandschuster.com

DEDICATION

This book is dedicated to my dear mother and my dear father, the two people who created such a wonderful and smart human being.

My dear mother, Theresa, you are my heart and my soul and the center of my world. I dedicate this book to you for showing me what the true meaning of life is. You have taught me what other mothers didn't. This book is dedicated to you for sticking by me through the ups and the downs in my life as well as my career. You and I have been through hell and back and I love and thank you for everything you are and everything that you will be. I also want to congratulate you on going back to school and obtaining your college degree. You are a strong and smart woman and I want to thank you for raising a strong and smart man. I promise you that before you close your eyes that your dreams will forever come true. We have been down a long road with a lot of bumps and now here's what the end feels like. I love you, Mom!

My dear father, Milton, whom God with His almighty wisdom took away from me too soon. I can never forget the times that we shared together while you were on this earth. Each and every day, I light a candle in remembrance of your strength and your power that was instilled into my brothers and me. Not a day goes by that a tear doesn't fall from my eye when I think of you. But I need to remind myself that you don't want me down here crying over your death. For you, I will hold my head up high and reach for the stars just like you said. The one thing that the MAN can't take away from you is your knowledge and Dad, I know you're watching over me using my brain each and every day. It's been very hard for me since you parted this earth but one thing I will remember is to always reach for the stars and I will always be your *Fat Boy*.

Daddy, R.I.P.

1953-2005

ACKNOWLEDGMENTS

First of all, I would like to give a special tribute to all of the people in my life that God has loaned and taken away from me. All of the people left a large scar on my heart and I will never forget all of the good times we shared. I love and miss you all.

Henry Ford Christmas
Luke Blackwell, Sr.
Milton Hall, Jr.
Tyrone Hall
Willie Rutledge
Emma Thompson
Anna May Gresham
Riley Williams
Ms. Holmes
Rasheeda Monroe
Cynthia Thompson
John Ritter
Will Notorious
Mike Notorious
Calvin Finney (55th ST)

You all may be missed but not forgotten.

Now let's get down to the nitty-gritty. You know, some people came at me sideways when they saw that their names weren't mentioned in *Smoking Cigarettes*. I'm here to tell you now, through these acknowledgments, if your names aren't mentioned or missed a certain criteria, that means that I don't know you or we don't get along. It's no beef, I'm just being real.

To my mother, here's to you, kid. Let's make a toast to financial freedom. It's about time and now it's time for your youngest son to shine. To my dad, RIP. You just keep watching over me guiding me in the right direction. I'M TRYING MY BEST.

To my grandmom Chicken, you have given more wisdom and help than one person could give in a lifetime. Even though your life is down in Atlantic City, I'll make sure that you get there every other day even if it means that I have to write ten books a month. I'll make sure that you get there at your free will.

To Grandma and Grandpa Hall, I would like to thank you for putting up with a grandson like me. I know I can be a handful. To my brothers, Rickey and Ralpheal, let's make sure that we take care of Mom together. Actually, it's her time to shine. To my husband, my best friend, my rock, Keyon, words cannot express the love and the patience that you've given me through the years. I would like to thank you for looking out for me when no one else would and I love you for the forever bond that we have that was tried and could never be broken. I know I have been putting you on the back burner while I deal with this book and talk-show but know that I love you and at the end, I'm the one that will have your back. Now that this book is done, you can have my full, undivided attention again. Let's have fun.

Sweet kisses to the one and only girl in my life Kaniyah

Macmillan, you are my heart and my soul and I cannot imagine a day with you.

Here, I gotz 2 give a shoutout to my crazy-azz fammilee. These people are the nuttiest set of folks on this side of the face of the earth but I wouldn't trade them for anything in the world.

Let me start off my thanking my aunts Diane and Gloria, Connie and Adrien and uncles Frank, Pop and Junie. Duke, I'll be glad when you bring ya azz home and stays home. Make this bid ya last. To my Uncle Pop, I'll be selling you a used car sometime soon. LOL!

To my super cousins, who stuck with me through thick and thin. Romona, congratulations on your wedding, your new baby and your new husband, Hezekiah. I wish you both nothing but happiness and joyful times together. Nicole, you have done a wonderful job in raising your children, Shaneera and Jahbriea. I wish that you continue your life happy and free as you can be. Stanley, what I need you to do is stay strong. Stay strong for your mother and your sister. Just be strong for yourself because as a family we will all get through this together. On that note I'd like to shoutout my cousins, Richard and kids, Anthony and his kids.

To my cousins Marquette and Tamora, I want to thank ya'll both for being there when I needed someone to talk to and giving some of the greatest advice. I'll always be honored. Along with that, shoutout to Camisha, Susan, Andre Jr. and Baby Eric, even though you're grown, you'll always be a baby to me. Hello, Andrea!

You haven't had a cheesesteak until you had one of my Uncle Andre's at Jim's Steaks.

To the best friend in the entire world, Dele. The Africans

haven't seen beauty until they've seen you. I cannot live this life without you so hold on, this will be a bumpy ride.

To Janyra and family. I thank you, girl, from the bottom of my heart for sticking by my side no matter what the cost is.

Miesha, a sophisticated lady! I can't even tell you how you got a spot on this page because you are never there when I need you. But one thing I can say is that you're always on time. And a ride-or-die CHICK at that and that's what a young man like me needs in his life. And shoutout to your new baby, ENOCH. LOL! Don't laugh, y'all, it's a cute name (I hate it) but it's a cute name. The Hudson family, I love all of you.

To my gay mother and father; every gay man should have a pair of these. Daniel and John. Thanks for the love and support that you both show me every day. I can't stop loving y'all if I tried. And on that note; I can't 4get my gay brothers—Rantonio; can't wait for the wedding! Hueshaun, Sam and Stephan.

Yo, I gotta get these damn haters off my back, damn! Anyway, sorry for the interruption, now where was I?

I see y'all peekin', thinking I forgot y'all but I didn't. My extended family; my baby boy Rondell, damn, I can't even call you that no more cuz you a grown man, dawg!

Ms. Debbie, Kaira (mother of the cutest set of twins on earth), Maishanna, Fatima, and Tyree.

A special shoutout to Robin and Jeff; when I find my special someone I would want our relationship to be just like y'all. To all my nephews; stay in school. I can't name 'em all cuz it could be more than I know of.

R.I.P. to the man that inspired me to write and stay focused. Malcolm Starks. You will always be remembered.

To the Best Publicist that money *can't* buy: Monique Ford. I would like to thank you for all your support and keeping me focused during the dark times of my life. God has sent you from heaven and for that we have grown to work together and I know that you will always be there even when everything else fails. Love you, girl! And to Nakea Murray, thanks for everything and I'm glad you did what you did to bring me out of my shy shell, love u lots.

A glorious thanks to my fairy godmother Carla for all the encouragement and willpower. You are truly someone that appears in a flash and thanks.

I would like to say thanks to Earl Cox for bringing me into this business to get started on my way.

Roll out the red carpet for Zane and Charmaine and their lovely associates. I thank God for the day when you walked through that lonely forest and tripped over that rock and found me. No one could have done it better. Thanks for believing me and seeing my worth. I won't let you down. I promise!

To KaShamba Williams and Daaimah S. Poole. I love y'all two beautiful women for passing on the knowledge that you've learned from this business to me. Daaimah, you're the only one who actually sat me down and took the time to HELP me; I will always be grateful for that. Also, I really want to give a special thanks to Vickie Stringer. You have taken my hand and guided me in the right direction and I'll bow down to you for that. Thanks!

I have 2 holla at my girl, the girl that could not have touched a piece of paper with a pen better. My big sister Brenda L. Thomas. You go, girl!

Speakin' of paper and pens—we're all in this 2gether. I come from a whole family of writers and there are a lot of us. What? You didn't know? Well, let me remind you Shawna Grundy—

I'll check you out at the buffet cuz you know how we can bust a grub, Alyce Thompson—I see you girl, Solomon Jones, Karen E. Quinones Miller, Azarel (you are soooo pretty. If only I was straight!), Hickson, Tracy Brown, Mister Man Frisby, Anna J, Marlene Taylor, Miasha, Asante Kahari, Elizabeth Gore, Tu-Shonda L. Whitaker, Shamora Renee, Chandell Bey, Nikki Turner, Shannon Holmes, Lynnette Khalfani, Lee Hayes, O. Salik-Evans, T.N. Baker, Eric Gray, Rikeem Wilburn, James Earl Hardy, Mark Anthony, and last but not least, my main man Brandon McCalla. Omarion, it was very nice meeting you. Stay real!

Treasure E. Blue & Kwan, you two men are the realest men I know. Treasure, stay on ya grind and you will be the next Donald Trump. Kwan, you are my dawg, stay real.

One Luv to my barber/stylist Niyru for keepin' me looking so fresh and so clean and the coolest Probation Officer in the game, Mary Ellen, shoutout to you for keeping my azz out of jail.

To all the bookstores that showed me love throughout my trying times: Ms. Betty and the entire staff at Ligourious Books, thanks so much for your support. Tyra at Borders Express at the Liberty Place. You know I'll shut shop down for you, girl. A special shoutout to Ms. Emelyn and her staff at Mejah Books in the Tri-State Mall in Delaware. Shoutout to Rita at Borders Express in the Gallery. And mad shouts to Cindy and the whole Staff at Waldenbooks in Long Island, N.Y., Emperiam Books (Tiffany and Zahir).

The radio stations; thanks for all your support, The Dreamteam (Power99), Golden Girl and Qdeezy. Tarsha (Jonesy aka Ms. Jones), Todd Lynn, DJ Envy, Miss Info, and the whole Hot97 staff. WHAT radio—the Wendy Williams Experience, thanks to the entire Experience staff, Power105, and Philly 1003 the beat. Shoutout to Joey Zaza.

To all the street vendors in NYC, thanks for pushing my books and helping to make my dreams come true—Che, Sidee, and Fatima.

Mad shoutouts to Thais, Cindy (congratulations, Grandmom), the Hudson family, I can't forget that crazy-ass Chezy and Bruce (the broke version of Whitney and Bobby), Darylisha, Jerome, Andre, Keith, Wayne, Grandpop, Mrs. Darlene, Robin, Pastor Ricky, Aunt Dar, Tony, Maxwell (crazy ass), Shon, Stevie (boo boo), Shauna, Tamika, Mel Jackson, Young Sir, Sharon, Pooh, Donnie, Neisha, Kyron, Terrence, Alisha and Rasul, Chuck, Keisha, Jorell, Job, Peaches, Tyrea, Diana, Jay-Z, Queen Pen, After 7, Omarion, Donnie Simpson, Kimora Lee Simmons, Charlie Mack and 215 Entertainment, Bow Wow, Dr. Al Mameniskis, Tracie, Gwen, Charles Burks, Jr., Deon, Robert Datner, and to all my readers all over—I thank y'all for the support, letters, e-mails, and the constant reviews. This is the second time around so here we go again. God bless to all and to all good night.

In Love With a *Thug*

Reginald L. Hall

PROLOGUE

I want a man who can sell salt to a slug
My only quest in life is to find a ruffneck or a thug
He has to walk around doing shit with no shame
He knows all about the streets and is knee deep in
the drug game
A thug who can't get enough of the girls and makes
lots of money
So he can give it all to me—his love—his true thug honey
My thug has all the power and walks through the streets
demanding respect
He comes home—I've cooked and cleaned.
I love the way he has me in check
Will I ever find a thug like this? I'm the one, so it seems
Or do I keep hoping this becomes reality instead of
having delusional wet dreams

—K. WEEMS

I

In the Shower

The water ran hot as it dripped down both our bodies as he kissed me passionately. Both of our dicks stood brick as we faced each other letting our precum mix as the water ran between us.

"I love you so much, Darnell," I said as he palmed my ass, pulling me closer to him to let our dicks smash between our bellies. Our tongues twisted with great divine as I grabbed his back and held tight, thinking of all the good times that we shared together. The hot water from the shower fogged up the mirrors and the steam flowed through the entire bathroom.

"Show me how much you love me," he said, kissing and licking all over my lips. I began kissing his neck as the hot water ran over my face and proceeded down to his chest where I sucked on his nipple while fingering the other. I felt his large penis poking me in my stomach as I continued to make him horny.

"Yeah, I like that shit," he said as he stood there with his head leaned back and his eyes closed. He began to lick his lips from left to right. I kneeled down, staring at his ten-and-a-half-inch dick pointing straight at me. His curly pubic hairs were getting curlier as the water tapped his body. His hairy balls hung looking so juicy and ripe when I began to taste the head of his cucumber. I started out by teasing him, hoping that he would clench from my licks and he did. I then downed his whole sausage into my mouth as his once-sagging balls became tight.

The hot water continued to hit my face as he grabbed my head from behind and began to fuck my face. He was throwing jabs at the back of my throat as he begun to move faster and faster. I grabbed his tight muscular butt cheeks to force him deeper into my mouth.

"Ayo, watch them hands, you know a nigga don't be letting people touch my ass. Keep sucking this dick. It's yours," he explained as he pumped himself tight into my mouth with me gagging at every stroke. I then pulled it out and licked it up and down slowly. I licked all around the head and sucked on his tip for about five minutes. That shit drove him crazy. He looked down at me and smiled as he kindly stuck his piece back into my mouth to continue sucking.

"Yo, eat this dick up. You gon' let me cum in ya mouth?" he asked, still long-stroking his muscle in and out my mouth. I looked up at him as I noticed him looking down at me, ready to go to work. I deep throated him quickly as I shook my head obligingly.

"Yeah, that's my boy. You like this dick, don't you?" he asked. I loved it when he talked dirty to me while we were having sex. I stroked my dick the whole time I sucked his. I grabbed the shaft of his muscle and licked it up and down like a lollipop as I sucked some more while jerking him at the same time. I was already starting to feel the tingling sensation in my dick so I knew that I needed to make this nigga bust a nut soon.

"C'mon, man, eat dat dick," he yelled as he placed both of his hands on the walls of the shower to brace himself for this lovely nut. When he would get loud, I knew that that was my cue to suck on it a little harder. The water continued to pour from the sprout as I jerked myself off and sucked him at the same time.

"Oh shit," he yelled as I felt all his semen rush from the shaft to the tip of his dick and into my mouth and down my throat. I then shot my load into the water that rushed down the drain.

"Damn, that shit felt good," he said as I got up from my knees and kissed my thug right in the mouth.

I wrapped both of my arms around him as the water drenched us both. He did the same as he kissed me on my neck.

"I love you so much, Darnell, I don't know what I would do without you," I said as I laid my head on his chest. My heart skipped a beat every time I would get mushy with him. This was only once in a blue moon because Darnell never went for that mushy shit.

My nigga was all about gettin' dat paper, smoking dro, and fuckin' the shit out of me. That's all he lived for and no matter how feminine I was or how flamboyant I dressed, he would let no one fuck with me.

"I love you too, boo. But, look, I need you to help me with a favor," he said, taking my chin and raising my head so my eyes could directly meet his. Our lips touched yet once again while the shower was running. The look in his eyes seemed so sincere that I would do anything for this man, even if it meant dying for this man.

"Wassup? What's wrong?" I asked with a puzzled look upon my face. We released from each other's arms as he grabbed the soap and the sponge from the dish and began washing my back and my arms.

"Nothing's really wrong. I need you to help me plan out a few things; that's all," he said, now taking the soapy sponge and wiping down the crack of my ass.

After making sure that my ass was squeaky clean, he then bent me over, letting my hands rest on the hot and cold knobs. He began eating my ass like he'd never eaten an ass before. I closed my eyes as my dick started to get hard again. I'd forgotten that he wanted to talk to me. After about ten minutes of ass eating, he was ready to put the head in, as if my sucking him off wasn't enough.

"Oh, Baby, that hurts," I said, trying to get my anus ready for the big size of his dick.

"C'mon, Baby, let Daddy in," he said as he squeezed his semi-hard penis into my anus. The water was running heavily down our two bodies as he started to bang me from one side of the bathtub to the other.

After he came for a second time, we both washed each other's bodies and wrapped ourselves in oversized towels. Before we walked out of the bathroom he grabbed me from behind, letting his softness rub up against my ass and making my dick hard for a third time.

"Thanks for the wash, Baby," he said, holding me tight from the back. His arms were so thick and I felt safe being wrapped inside them.

"It was my pleasure. Thanks for the relaxation," I rebutted. I smeared the steam from the mirror with my hand, exposing my caramel face with his dark-skinned one as he stood directly behind me.

I opened the medicine cabinet to get my deep cream moisturizer for my face, then began applying it as he watched me. I stopped.

"What? What are you looking at?" He stood about six feet one with his chocolate-covered biceps.

"Nothing," he said, talking with his hands. "I want to know why you're putting all that stuff on your face. I mean, you look good the way you are."

I smiled from ear to ear. "Oh, Darnell, thank you. That was so nice of you to say," I said, giving him a kiss on his lips, then hopping back in front of the mirror. He then went into the room as I stood in front of the mirror gazing at my reflection. I started thinking of my future and how I would like to own my own hair salon one day. *But the way these bills are kicking my ass now, I know that that day will never happen.*

"Juan, why are you looking like that?" Darnell asked. He ran back in the bathroom in his wife beater and boxers. Still, I didn't take my eyes off my reflection in the mirror. "What are you thinking about?"

"Darnell, do you know what my dream is?" I asked him as he came behind me and started to rub my shoulders.

"Yes, Juan, I do know what your dream is."

"Well, what is it then?" I teased.

"I know that someday you want to have a shop of your own," he said.

I turned around and smiled giving him a great big hug.

We walked into my bedroom where he grabbed the sheets from the bed and uncovered two nine-millimeter handguns lying side by side with a red rose in the middle. My heart dropped. I turned toward his direction.

"Darnell, why are these guns on my bed and where did they come from?" I asked, totally confused.

"Juan, this was the favor I needed your help with. Baby, I need your help to rob a bank."

My eyes lit up full of rage at the thought of helping him rob a bank. "Darnell, I don't know shit about robbing no damn banks," I yelled. "Who the fuck do you think I am?" I asked before his backhand threw me across the room.

I landed on the other side of the bed and began holding my jaw. The sting from his slap took my mind off the thoughts of my future when he came rushing over to me.

"Get up," he said with red eyes. I got up to stare him straight in his face, still holding on to my jaw. He grabbed both of my shoulders and guided me toward the bed where we both sat down.

"Now, first of all, you're going to lower your voice. Second, you said that there was nothing that you wouldn't do for me." I began to get scared because I had known what Darnell was capable of. The last time he and I had gotten into a fight, he'd slapped me on the face with an unopened beer can. It was only because I had wanted to go out with my friends to a party. But, of course, he declined as always.

"I do love you," I said, massaging my jaw. He picked up the rose and placed it between my fingers.

"Well, Baby, if you love me, you will do this for me. Listen, I'm tired of being broke and not being able to take you to the places that you want to go. I feel bad sometimes because I can't afford to get you the finer things in life. Baby, you deserve that. You deserve to have a man that can take care of you. That's why I need you to help me to do this." I held the rose up to my nose and took a deep sniff as a tear fell down the left side of my cheek.

"Darnell, I would do anything for you but I don't think I can rob a bank. I'm a Christian and I have morals," I explained.

"Baby, that Christian mess went out the window with this gay shit." He gritted. "If there was ever a time where I needed you, this is the time. Baby, please, I'm begging you. We need to do this for us." I held the rose to my nose again but this time I closed my eyes and took a longer sniff. "Juan, you won't have to do anything. I'll plan everything and all you have to do is be by my side and play the wifey role. I swear, Baby, I'll take care of you," he said, looking deep into my eyes.

I stared into his eyes.

"Baby, what do you need me to do?"

II
BLOODY MONEY

Friday, January 14, 2005
12:41 p.m.

"Get the fuck down," yelled Darnell as he stomped his Timberland boot in the back of the white lady's neck and pointed the gun at her head. All I could hear were loud screams that clouded me from hearing anything that went on around me.

"Bitch, you heard him, now move," I yelled to another white woman when Darnell jumped behind the teller station and grabbed yet another woman who seemed to be expecting a child. As Darnell yanked her up by her hair she screamed with fear.

"Shut the fuck up, bitch," spat Darnell as he continued to struggle with the pregnant woman before he threw her to the floor.

My heart began pounding a mile a minute because I had never done anything like this. I often heard the saying that you have to be down for your man but I never knew that it involved robbing a bank. My hand was shaking faster and faster as I held my nine-millimeter handgun to the customer's head. I glanced up at the clock on the wall of the Commerce Bank on Eighteenth and Walnut streets that read 12:45. I knew that in minutes the po-po would be here.

"Fuck that," yelled Darnell from behind the teller station when

I heard two shots ring out and another woman scream. I saw the branch manager's body hit the floor. A fifty-six-year-old African-American female who probably had a husband and three kids with two in college and one in the Army; she never saw it coming.

"Yo, Jay, grab the bag, nigga," demanded Darnell as I continued to stand in the same spot terrorized. I could not believe what I was seeing. The love of my life had shot and possibly killed someone in front of me. I continued to shake as I ran over to grab the bag from him.

"Here, take this. I'ma go in the back and see if I see some more shit. Shoot the muthafuckin' cameras," he said, tossing the bag into my arms. Out of instinct, I turned my aim toward the security cameras and shot each lens out, watching the shattered glass fall to the floor.

"That's my dawg," said Darnell, grabbing his member with one hand and holding the gun in the other. I could tell he was smiling, even through his black ski mask. Looking at my man in that sense made me hot.

In the bank, five people lay with their chests tightly to the floor, scared for their lives. My face started to dampen from the wool ski mask that covered my identity. I took a step back to take note of the place in split seconds to find people crying, desks overturned, papers everywhere, and the last thing Darnell and I needed to hear were police sirens.

"Ayo, D," I yelled out toward the back room as I continued to point my gun at a few heads that popped up to see what was going on. By any means necessary I was gonna help my nigga get this loot.

"All right, everybody, I'm gonna leave this muthafucka in

silence," said Darnell, coming from the back room with another bag full of money. A tear began to roll down my face as I saw the dead body lying on the floor like something from a horror film. "I'ma need everybody to stay down on the floor and remain there until we leave this muthafucka."

As each minute counted down to each second the four walls of this financial center were closing in tighter and tighter on me. I wanted all of this to be over but I knew what I needed to do in order to be a ride-or-die for my nigga.

"Aight, J, let's go," he demanded. For some strange reason I couldn't move. My feet were stuck in one spot. "Are you deaf, nigga? I said, let's go." He grabbed the back of my coat and I yelled, which triggered more screams from the customers and the one pregnant bank teller. The police sirens got louder.

"Nigga, if we get caught, that's gonna be ya ass. Now let's go."

I snapped out of my trance and began to run in the same direction as him. My body tensed up and my mind started going crazy. It seemed like I was running in one spot. Was this all a dream? I couldn't move. All I heard were police sirens that drowned the sound of Darnell screaming my name. I stood motionless.

"Fuck," Darnell screamed as he glanced out of the front picture window and saw a cop car graze the sidewalk. He quickly turned around and began running toward me, charging for the back door, when I heard a loud pop sound. The sound echoed again and, this time, Darnell fell face forward onto the floor.

Darnell's grunts sounded severe as I dropped to my knees and grabbed his head. People were still lying on the floor, covering themselves with their hands over their heads. My heart melted almost immediately as I saw the love of my life cough up blood, trying to hold on to his life.

"Darnell, can you hear me, Baby?" I asked as I removed his ski mask. "Please, Baby, don't leave me. Get up. We have to go," I cried out. A few steps away from us stood a black gray-haired security guard who tried to gain control of the situation by filling my man with two bullets. I could tell that he was working on releasing the third bullet but this time I was his target.

I reached down beside Darnell's body and grabbed his gun without hesitation and filled the guard's body with three bullets. I watched his body jerk back and forth a couple times before it went totally limp. All I heard were women screaming and Darnell's sense of holding on. I threw the gun back on the floor once I saw that the guard was no longer moving.

"Oh, my God, what have you done?" I screamed as the other people in the bank watched me like a hawk to see is I was still indeed trigger-happy. My ski mask soaked all my tears as I bent over to give Darnell one last kiss on his bloody lips. My body shook with agony and fear of not knowing what was gonna happen next. I closed my eyes as tight as I could as nostalgia went through my mind.

How could the person with whom I shared my dreams of life be slipping away from my arms? I rocked his body back and forth as I continued to hear the police sirens draw nearer. I got up and grabbed both of the black trash bags full of money.

The sun that shone brightly through the windows of the bank when we first walked in didn't seem so bright anymore. I looked around at everyone's face one last time before I fled to the back area where the bank tellers were. I pushed the chairs out of the way and stepped over the bank manager's body, which lay face forward on the floor. Her black hair with red streaks covered her face.

"Do you have a back door?" I screamed to the pregnant teller who didn't know whether to answer me. She stood there in total shock as I noticed her crooked nametag, which read "Michelle Smith." "I said, do you have a back door?" I yelled again but this time retrieving my loaded nine-millimeter and pointing it directly at her head.

"Yes, it's right through there," she said, motioning in the direction of the employee lounge. Without saying another word, I turned and ran toward the back area past a kitchen where a television and a microwave sat on the counter. Once I arrived at the door that read "Emergency Exit Only," I forcefully kicked the entire door open as the alarms flooded my ears in all different directions. I held both bags tight toward my chest and ran as fast as I could through the alleyway and onto the busy street.

As I made my way toward the intersection at Rittenhouse Square, I saw what seemed like the entire police force bombarding the financial center. My running then became a slow walk as I carried myself, the two bags of money, and my memories of Darnell into the sunlight.

III

BUT THE BIG STORY ON ACTION NEWS TONIGHT...

Friday, January 14, 2005
6:00 p.m.

"The most watched news around the Delaware Valley with your hosts—Lisa Thomas Laury and Rick Williams—here's Channel 6 Action news."

"A fire erupted in a North Philadelphia home tonight, Osama Bin Laden is still on the loose, and author Reginald L. Hall is still continuing to sell millions of books all across the country. But the big story on Action News tonight is what started as a routine bank robbery that ended with three homicides. Denise James is live on the scene at the Commerce Bank at Eighteenth and Walnut with the full story. Denise."

"Good evening, Rick, that is correct. I am down here at the Commerce Back at Eighteenth and Walnut where this branch was robbed earlier today. Not only is this a crime scene for a robbery but this is a scene where not one but three people were murdered during the robbery. The victims include bank security guard John McCants, a fifty-five-year-old from Chester, Pennsylvania; Darnell Rhodes, twenty-five of West Philadelphia, one of the said gunmen in this treacherous shootout; and branch manager Beverly Vaughn, fifty-four of Southwest Philadelphia.

"Some of the customers were taken to University Hospital

for medical treatment. From my understanding there is still another gunman on the loose. Bank officials confirm that there is one suspect remaining at large—sources say that the gunman got away with about one hundred fifty-thousand dollars. Live from Commerce Bank at Eighteenth and Walnut streets, Denise James with Channel 6 Action News."

IV
CHÉ MYSTIC

Friday, May 27, 2005
10:55 p.m.

"I hope that these bitches don't think they'll be dressed better than me at my grand opening of my muthafuckin' salon," I said to Anthony on the phone as I laid my clothes on the bed that I'd bought earlier that day.

"Well, what are you going to wear? I hope that it's not gonna be nothing too feminine or flashy."

"Bitch, I know your ass ain't talkin' 'bout nuffin' too feminine or flashy. Not as much as you be out there shaking your ass with those niggas from the Five Spot with those tight clothes on," I spat as we both started to giggle.

"Whatever, you're jealous because I'm stunning and I'm gonna turn your own party out tonight when I come up in there with my Diesel jeans on and my Lucky fitted shirt only buttoned halfway. Muthafuckas is not even gonna know your name," Anthony said, laughing.

Anthony and I had been friends for the past ten years. I met him when I was graduating from high school in Germantown. I knew he was gay from the first time I saw him. He thought he was fooling people because he was high-yellow with braids and a tight body and all the girls were on him. But when he came up to me and complimented me on my Prada man bag, I knew right then and there that he was a queen.

And ever since then we were close and, as the years went by, he became fruitier and fruitier, and the fruitier he got the wilder he would get. He never kept a steady boyfriend. He would have sex day in and day out but his heart would only beat for one man and that was this boy whom he loved named Darrell. Darrell was a straight guy that would only fuck around with Anthony behind his girl's back. Anthony did admit that he only liked him a lot because of his thug demeanor; not to mention his long curtain rod that was used for things other than hanging curtains. And even though Darrell would tell Anthony all the time that all he ever wanted was sex Anthony stayed at his beck and call.

There was nothing I could do but shake my head. Anthony was my dawg but I wished he didn't have sex with different people so damn much.

"We'll see, bitch. I gotta go because my ride will be here in a few to pick me up. I'll see you in the ride and your outfit better be fresh enough to walk the red carpet," I said before the line went dead.

I placed the phone on its base with a lot of excitement that had been built up in me ever since I went to settlement on my own salon. I couldn't believe that this day was finally gonna come. Something that I had always dreamed about and now it was finally coming to reality. *Ché Mystic, it's about time.*

Walking around my pink-colored room I hurried to my dresser to choose what scent of cologne I would wear tonight. This was the event of all events for Philadelphia. I made sure that I put all my networking skills to the test for tonight's event. The grand opening of Ché Mystic. Who'd have thought? It was a good thing that my uncle worked as Will Smith's agent so he was able to get me in touch with all the top heads in Philly. Most of them would be able to bless me with their presence this evening.

At first it was kind of hard getting a VIP area set up in a hair salon but I pulled it off. I had to make sure Mr. Smith and his lovely wife had somewhere to sit and sip their champagne. Tonight's event would be hosted by none other than Power 99's "Golden Girl" and Allen Iverson. My night would be set and I couldn't wait.

I hurried into the bathroom and readied my shower. As the steam from the hot water filled the bathroom I gently rubbed my body down with some body butter from Victoria's Secret before I knelt by my bedside to say my evening prayers.

Dear Lord,

I am coming to you at this time to say thank You. I want to thank You for all Your many blessings in life that You have provided me with. I also want to ask You to please forgive me for my sins. And dear Lord, can you please take care of Darnell and watch over him in Your kingdom. I know if it wasn't for him this all wouldn't be possible. Thank you. Amen.

I got up and went over to my dresser where my mirror sat with many pictures. I grabbed the picture of Darnell and closed my eyes and kissed the Polaroid as if I were kissing his soft lips. I removed the dead rose that sat on my dresser and sniffed it as if it were still new. I stood in the middle of my bedroom holding onto a picture that held so many memories of my life with Darnell. There would never be another who would take his place.

Many emotions built up inside of me as my eyes started to tear. The pain that his family felt during his passing would never gain the significance of any of the pain that I felt. Darnell was the Clyde to my Bonnie. Although technically I am not a female, I was his bitch and he was my nigga. The emotions continued to build as I pondered my thought of the countless nights that we made love and the early mornings when he would get me aroused in my sleep and break me off before he went back on the block.

Darnell was not merely my lover; he was my friend, my protector. I always knew that Darnell would take care of business and that there was no need for me to worry. He took care of me until his dying day and made sure that all was well with me before his heart stopped beating. He bled over my money and, for that, I would always appreciate him. The phone rang and snapped me out of my trance. I kissed the picture one last time before wiping my eyes clean.

"Hello," I greeted.

"What are you doing?" Ieshia asked. "I hope you're gonna be ready by the time the limo gets there."

"I'm trying to hurry up. I was about to get in the shower before you called. Are you gonna be ready?" I asked, walking down the hall and into my kitchen to fix myself a glass of wine to hold me over until the party.

"Yes, I'm already dressed. You know I've been excited. I got on my best whore's dress cuz me and Antwoine is gonna turn the place out," she said, laughing.

"Oh, I didn't know you was bringing Antwoine. He doesn't have duty tonight?"

"Yeah, he did work today but he got off early. Now you know

my man is not gonna pass up a night of free drinks," she said as we both chuckled about her man.

"Well, you go ahead with your navy man. Look, I gotta go if I'm gonna be on time. I'll see you in the ride."

"Okay."

"Bye."

I put the cordless back on the base and took another long sip of wine before I proceeded to the shower. After letting the water run for about fifteen minutes it was sweaty hot; just the way I like it.

I jumped in the shower and stood under the running water letting the steady stream drown out my troubles. Instead of my mind being filled with the excitement of finally opening my own hair salon, it was covered by the burden that wailed on my mind over Darnell's death. Oh, how I wished that we would have done something else that day instead of robbing that bank.

Things would have been so much different if we would have used our brains. My baby still would've been here and I would not be feeling the emptiness that lay in my heart.

After showering and lotioning my body with palm oil from my favorite place, Victoria's Secret, I greased my scalp thoroughly before giving my hair the extra twist I needed to make it look sharp for this occasion. I stood naked in the mirror running my fingers through my hair as it hung gracefully to my shoulders. I always admired my own smile, the same way Darnell would. For starters, I was very much in love with my body and knew how to work every inch of it to get the things I wanted.

I had worked very hard for my flat stomach. Well, you might as well say I worked hard for it. I had to actually work to find the right plastic surgeon for a tummy tuck. That's hard work.

Chile, I was on it and once I had the finances to get it done, I was gone. I winked at my caramel complexion one last time before I dressed.

About a half-hour later the car was downstairs. Now the excitement was starting to set in. My outfit was on point. I had put the last coat of clear nail polish on my nails before the receptionist from downstairs called to let me know that my ride was waiting. I put the finishing touches on my outfit with a dirty-brown corduroy Armani blazer. added a little blush on my cheeks, and I was out the door.

I walked out of the building on Presidential Boulevard with stares from white people of all ages as the chauffeur opened the door for my entrance.

"Well, it's about time, bitch," said Anthony who had already taken it upon himself to pop the Crissy before I got in.

"And whose party is it anyway?" I said, snatching his glass from him and placing it to my lips. "It's mine so I'll be the one to drink first."

"Where am I going now, sir?" asked the Caucasian gentleman who drove the limo.

"You're gonna make a left at this next light. We need to pick up Ieshia," I said, still trying to down my glass.

"How does it feel to be opening your hair salon finally?" asked Anthony. "I mean you don't look like you're that happy about it," he continued.

"I'm happy. It's just that I wish Darnell could be here to share it with me, you know?" I said as I downed another sip of the Cris.

"You actin' as if y'all were together for a long time. You only knew him for about three months. Juan, how in the hell did you get hooked on him that fast?" he asked, talking with his hands.

"It's easy to fall in love with someone in three months. Don't act like you've never done it."

"See, that's why I hate fucking with faggots. You meet someone one minute, then fall for them the next," he spat. "This nigga didn't even care about you and now he's dead and you're walking around here all depressed and shit."

"Excuse me for falling in love with a guy and not using him strictly for sex like you do," I rebutted. "And what makes you so sure that he really didn't care for me, huh?"

"Well, I would think if he did, then he wouldn't have put you in danger by robbing a fuckin' bank, now would he?" he said, looking directly into my eyes as we both got silent. "I rest my case," he continued as he began pouring himself another glass of Cristal.

"I can't believe you said that shit," I spat, getting heated. "You were not supposed to ever throw that in my face."

"Juan, the creep is dead and you're walking around here feeling sad, like that muthafucka was God's gift to a fuckin' faggot. He treated you like crap. Your ass could be in jail right now. Or better yet, dead, and not to mention he cheated on you with three of your friends and you acting like it was all love."

"No, fuck that. We are gonna forget about him and go to your grand opening and I really don't want you to bring his name up no more this evening. Okay?"

I sat there feeling like a scolded child. "Okay, I guess you're right. This *is* my night and I should be happy." I sat back and raised the glass to my lips.

"Now that's more like it," he said, extending his arms for a hug.

I rolled the tinted window down halfway to get some of that night air as we pulled in front of Ieshia's door. Her mother stood in the doorway smiling as the car rode up and double-parked in the street.

"Hey, Juan," she screamed from the door in an all-white terry-cloth robe. "I'm so sorry I can't be at your party tonight. I have a terrible cold."

"That's okay, Ms. Jones," I replied. "I'll have Ieshia bring you a plate."

"Thanks," she said as Ieshia slightly brushed past her sporting a black dress that stopped at her knees and showed much cleavage.

"Alright, girl," yelled Anthony from the window. Ieshia then went into her black handbag and pulled out her Chanel glasses and placed them over her eyes.

"Now we can go," she said, smiling ear to ear, showing off her voluptuous cocoa-colored body as the chauffeur got out and walked around to let her in. I had already begun to pour her a drink as she placed her rump comfortably on the seat.

"Where's Antwoine?" I asked, handing her the champagne glass.

"Oh, he says that he's gonna meet us there." She reached over to Anthony and gave him a four-arm hug. "How are you doing, Baby?" she greeted. "Watch your hair. I don't wanna spill my drink."

With the three of us in the back of the car, we shared love and drank the Cris and we were all the way live.

$$$$$

Chris Brown's song "Run It" was playing loud through the speakers of the limo when we turned the corner of Fifteenth and South streets near Broad. The stadium lights shone brightly as I sat by the tinted window and watched people walk into the salon.

I reached into my man bag and pulled out my shades to hide my tipsy eyes.

"Are you ready?" Anthony asked, still sipping his drink. My emotions hurried around in the pit of my stomach as my eyes started to tear; not from the excitement of the situation at hand but from the emptiness that I felt inside. I watched men palm their ladies at the lower part of their backs and the happiness that dressed their faces.

Tonight's event was on and poppin.'

"I'm as ready as I'm ever gonna be," I answered, not turning my face from the crowd. South Street was packed. There were cars that stood in the middle of the street that cost more than my salon. The town was settled and the music was mellow.

My uncle was not playing any games when he'd said that he'd make this a night to remember. Along with the cars, South Street was also decked with wall-to-wall limousines. I sat back as I watched Toni Braxton and her husband, Kerri, rush inside the salon. Busta Rhymes stood on the sidewalk talking to a slew of females. I watched Foxy Brown walk inside wearing a pair of skintight jeans and dark sunglasses.

Only if Darnell were here to see this. The chauffeur got out the car and walked inside the salon as Anthony, Ieshia, and I waited patiently. My heart began to beat as the chauffeur came back out with "Golden Girl" following behind. She sported blonde hair and a striped jumpsuit and held a microphone. He came up to the door and opened it as Anthony stepped out and walked the red carpet as if he owned it. Ieshia then took the stand, showing all her pearly whites as Allen Iverson grabbed her hand and escorted her inside. I held my breath for a split second and then made my exit from the vehicle.

"And here he is, the entrepreneur of the evening. The founder and CEO of Ché Mystic. *Ms. Thang*, Juan Jiles." I looked in the air as the fireworks started and "Golden Girl" grabbed my hand. The speakers blew heavily, playing Diana Ross' "I'm Coming Out" as people who stood on each side of the red carpet clapped in the distance. Cameras were flashing with nonstop pictures. I grabbed the opening of my blazer with both hands and walked down the carpet in stride.

Lending my hand and cheek for people to kiss made me feel so warm on the inside. Once inside the salon there were tables lined up against the wall covered with hors d'oeuvres from grapes and strawberries to crackers, wine and cheese. There were people from all over the area waiting for my arrival. People, both gay and straight, were waiting for me to walk into *my shop*. I went straight back to the VIP area where Toni Braxton and Wendy Williams sat discussing different types of hair extensions.

I looked over in the corner to see Chili from TLC sitting on the loveseat. She held a glass of champagne as she looked as stunning as ever, wearing an off-the-shoulder cream top, dark-blue jeans, and open-toe sandals.

"Hey, Juan," she said, standing and kissing both of my cheeks. I grabbed her hand and blushed innocently as she stood with a fine gentleman in tow. "Juan, this is my friend Ralph." I lightly let her hand go and grabbed his as he placed my hand gently to his lips and kissed the back. I could feel his neatly trimmed mustache tickle the back of my hand. This man was dark and debonair and, if I wasn't mistaken, he looked sort of like Bryce Wilson.

"He owns Platinum Sheers Hair Salon in Manhattan," continued Chili, leaning over into my ear. "I told him I was coming to your opening and he flipped. He's been dying to meet you."

Instantly my blood went from warm to a simmer sizzle and I began to blush as he gazed directly into my eyes.

"It's nice to finally meet you," he said in a deep voice that complemented his style. "I've seen your work in the latest issue of *Hype Hair* magazine. Words cannot describe your feminine style," he continued.

"Juan, Baby, I'll be over here if you need me," said Chili as she made her way to the front of the salon, leaving Ralph and me alone to talk.

"So how long have you been doing hair?" he asked, taking a sip of his drink.

"Well, I've been doing hair since I was fifteen but I always wanted to open my own shop."

"Well, congratulations, it's here." He smiled and raised his drink in the air.

"Thanks," I said, noticing my mouth starting to get dry as Anthony grabbed my arms from behind.

"Juan, I have someone I want you to meet," Anthony whispered into my ear, trying hard for me to hear him over the loud music. I cleared my throat. "Oh, excuse me. I didn't know that I was interrupting something," Anthony said as he did a double-take at Ralph. "Hi, I'm Anthony, and you are?" he said, extending his hand to Ralph.

"I'm Ralph," he answered, shaking Anthony's hand.

"I'm sorry, can I borrow him for a second?" Anthony said. I put on a phony smile for a minute.

"Um, excuse me for a second." I motioned to Ralph. "This better be important," I spat to Anthony.

"It is, bitch. Guess who's here? Ricky's cousin. Remember, I told you about him?"

"Yeah, and?"

"He's here. Let me introduce you to him," Anthony said excitedly as he rushed me to the back area where I planned for my office.

"Reggie, this is my best friend Juan," Anthony excitedly introduced us.

"Hi, how are you," said Reggie as we shook hands.

"I'm fine," I said, smiling and wishing he would let my hand go.

"It's so nice to meet you after hearing Ant talk about you all the time," he said, smiling. He finally let my hand go as he placed his hand gently to the lower part of Anthony's back.

"I'm glad you could make it to my party. Have fun," I said, still holding a phony smile, hoping to break away from those two nuts so I could get back to Ralph. I walked back to the area where Ralph and I were introduced and he was gone. As a matter of fact most of the people were gone from that area. It seemed like all of the action was drawn toward the front door. I could no longer hear music but what I did hear the sound of glass breaking and yelling from a high-pitched voice.

My heart fell to the pit of my stomach as I ran toward the entrance with Anthony following behind me. DJ Jay-Ski was packing up his equipment. I finally reached the entrance where I saw the flashing blue and red police lights. My guests were dashing to their cars. South Street was filled with Bentleys, Mercedes-Benzes, and limousines. I began focusing on the subject in front of me, who I knew to be Ieshia, screaming and her dress was torn.

"Pussy, I knew you was gay all the time," she yelled, running down the street with one shoe on and the other in her hand. I ran over to her and grabbed her from behind.

"Ieshia, what's wrong?" I asked, catching my breath and trying to hold her at the same time.

"Antwoine. That nigga was gay all the time," she repeated. Antwoine was now at the other end of the street running alongside Ralph.

"Calm down and tell me what happened," I said, still trying to get her situated.

"Are you okay, sir?" asked the black male cop who tried to help me calm her without succeeding.

"Yes, sir. I have her," I said, still trying to get ahold of her clothes so her breasts wouldn't show.

"Well, she needs to calm down; if not, I'll have to take her in," the officer stated firmly.

"Yes, sir. I am the owner of the salon."

"So, this was *your* party?" he asked.

"Yes," I said as he shook his head from side to side and walked away. It had begun to rain. "Anthony, can you go inside and make sure everything is okay while I take care of her?"

"Sure," he said, walking backward inside the salon.

The rain was now coming down steadily as the people started to scatter along South Street.

"Now, Ieshia, tell me what happened."

She started to speak through her tears and the rain that was splashing on her face caused her mascara to run. She took a couple of deep breaths to get herself together, then began to explain as I walked her over to the sidewalk and onto the red carpet.

"Antwoine came in the salon and when I went over to greet him, he told me to hold up a minute. Then he walked past me and went to whisper something in the guy's ear; that guy you were talking to earlier." She let out a big scream. Her tears were starting to fall rapidly.

"It's okay, it's okay," I said, grabbing her hand. "Continue."

"Both of them went into the bathroom so I waited for them right outside the door. Then someone came out of the bathroom. That's when I saw them through the mirror; tongue-kissing. So, I ran in there and broke them up and they laughed at me. I hit Antwoine and that's when he and the boy came outside and I ran after him. Four fucking years I've been with him," she continued. She buried her head in my chest, continuing to sob.

"I know, calm down. It's gonna be okay," I said, rubbing the back of her hair and letting her exhale her emotions for the both of us. All the tears that I wanted to let out but couldn't were falling from her eyes and the sky. I grabbed her head and held it tight against my chest. I stood there with my lonely thoughts as I consoled my friend. *Ralph was a cutie. Damn, why couldn't I have fucked him first?*

V

The Answer is You

Getting over a hangover was never the thing for me. I jumped up quicker than I should have when the phone rang. Intense pain rushed to the forefront of my head from the too many drinks I'd had last night at my party. I had to squint my eyes tight to block my pupils from the bright sun that shone through the miniblinds from my window. I peered throughout the room, looking at the clothes that were thrown on the floor from the previous night. Ieshia slept comfortably and was still in her clothes in the lounge chair that sat in the corner of my room. I pulled back the plush covers and stood up to stretch, letting my hard dick extend freely from my boxers. I went into the bathroom to take my morning piss.

I stood thinking of how exciting it was gonna be for Ché Mystic, its first day for business. I opened the medicine cabinet and popped two Tylenol to help get rid of my excruciating headache. Looking in the mirror, my hair was still intact as I smiled at myself. If that whole stunt with Ieshia hadn't gone down last night, I would have woken up with a cutie by my side.

"Wake up, sleepy head," I said, walking back into my bedroom and turning on the TV. "Would you like some coffee?" I asked her as she began to squirm.

"Sure, what time is it?" she asked with her eyes still closed.

I looked up at the alarm that sat on my forty-seven-inch television. "It's seven thirty. I have to get myself together for today," I said, getting up and walking out of the room into the kitchen to start the coffee.

"Juan, I have to ask you something," Ieshia yelled from the bedroom. I placed the coffee beans into the container and turned on the machine and walked back into the bedroom.

"Wassup?" I sat on the bed as she got up and walked over to me and sat beside me.

"I have to ask you for your help. I am hoping that you say yes," she said, turning to face me.

"Yeah, what's wrong? You know I will help you in any way that I can. Is something wrong?" I asked again.

"It's really not that big of a deal. First of all, I need some help getting some of my things from Antwoine's apartment."

"Okay, I'll help you with that. That's not a big deal," I responded.

"And, also I wanted to know if you could hire me to work in your shop?" She looked directly into my eyes. I quickly swallowed my spit because *that* I was not expecting.

"Ieshia. What happened to your job at the hospital? You are the best RN around here," I said, getting up and walking over to the lounge chair and having a seat.

"I know. But last week my supervisor tested my urine and it came back dirty," she said, looking down at the floor.

"Why the hell are you just telling me this? Why you didn't tell me last week when it first happened?"

"I don't know. Please don't yell at me. I'm so stressed right now. I can't take this shit," she responded with a shaken voice and teary eyes. Her tears began to fall down her cheeks.

"This all is happening too fast. I don't know what to do," she said, putting her head down and sobbing. I glanced down at the floor, then began twisting my hair around my finger. I got up, went back over to her and sat down on the bed.

"Calm down, Ieshia. I will help you." I grabbed her shoulder and squeezed. "It's gonna be okay. Don't worry." I sighed. "What type of experience do you have with hair?"

"I know how to do everything from weaves, curls, to extensions," she answered, still sniffing.

"Well, right now, I'm fully staffed but I'll tell you what. I'll let you start out as a shampoo girl and when a chair opens you can have it."

She turned to me and gave me the biggest hug. "Juan, thanks so much. I really do appreciate it," she said, continuing to hug me without letting go.

"Don't worry about it. You're gonna pull through this, baby girl," I said, noticing it was time for me to get dressed to head out.

Before heading to the salon I stopped at the Chinese people of Woodland Avenue to get my nails and feet done. I needed something to help soothe all the bullshit that seemed to be surrounding me. I reached in my man bag and grabbed my cell phone to dial Anthony. Of course he didn't answer his phone. Knowing him, he probably was still hung over from last night and was lying in his bed under Reggie's armpits.

I pulled up in front of Ché Mystic, letting my brand-new shiny 2005 gold Lexus be the center of South Street's attention. With my sunglasses palming my face I got out, letting the bright sun burn the top of my head as I walked over to unlock the door.

Rob was heading up the street wearing a pair of skin-tight jeans. He had his hair in a ponytail, carrying his man bag as if it was a pocketbook on a natural woman. His dark skin tone glimmered in the sun as he proceeded to walk toward me, smiling. The thickness of his body made his clothes extra tight. Rob was no slouch, though. He had graduated from The Philadelphia School of Hair and he knew damn well what he was doing. Weighing in at about 266 pounds of solid body, he would walk foot and eyewear off any given day for the House of Karan.

Rob was a six-time foot-and-eyewear winner for the House of Karan's Philly chapter. The House of Karan is one of Philadelphia's most respected homosexual gangs, better known as a "house." A house is a better way of saying "I am in a gang" from a gay person's point of view. Normally a house is run by two people, better known as the mother and the father, and all of their members are their children. Every other month or so the house will throw a big extravagant ball to showcase how fierce or how stylish their members are. The ball may consist of forty to fifty competition categories, sometimes maybe sixty.

These categories may include the prettiest face or the fiercest body or who can vogue the best. Personally I'm a member of the House of Labuchi. I'm legendary for my face and all the faggots know that I'm the one to be reckoned with. I joined the House of Karan when I was a young buck. I was only seventeen years old when I finally told my mother that my father traded dollars to me for sex favors. After I explained all that had happened, she called me a habitual liar and threw me out. With nowhere to go, I moved in with a boy I knew from school who lived with his father.

Come to find out that my father only wanted sex from me so I moved in with Tyrell Karan. Tyrell Karan was the father of what is known today as the Legendary House of Karan. He took me in as if I were his own. We lived in the heart of North Philly and he made sure that I ate and went to school each day.

Through unfortunate circumstances, Tyrell passed away when I was eighteen. I joined the House of Labuchi and I've been a member ever since.

By the time of Tyrell's passing I was a known spectacle in the ballroom scene. I was known for my nice grade of hair and my good looks. Whenever there was a ball coming to town I would strut my stuff on the runway and win. Sometimes I won gigantic trophies and other times I would win money, up to a thousand dollars. The ballroom scene was my life and sometimes it still is. I love all the colors, and the flashiness of the drag queens and how they perform on stage. I even thought about starting my own house one day but now that I'm running my own shop, I don't have the time.

"Hey, girl," said Rob as he sauntered his way in front of the shop with the straight boys on the corner looking on. He gave me a kiss on the cheek.

"Are you ready to do some heads?" I said, still smiling and greeting him.

"Yeah, girl, how many appointments do we have today?" he asked, waiting for me to remove the bulky lock from the door.

"I really don't know offhand but I know we're gonna be real busy." I finally got the lock off the door as we both went inside. The cleaning crew that I had hired really did a good job, considering the way it looked last night. The chairs were neatly shined with not a curler or curling iron out of place. Rob went into the back to get some supplies and then began to set up his station. I stood in the middle of the floor and took in the entire scene of the shop for a moment. Precious African-American art hung on the walls on one side while crystal clear mirrors hung on the other.

"Looks beautiful, doesn't it?" Rob said, walking to his station with his arms full of hair grease, styling gel, and holding spray.

"Yeah, I am flabbergasted." I smiled and looked around the room as if I was in another world. I walked to the back area and into my office where I stopped and stood back admiring my cherrywood desk and leather chair. There was wall-to-wall carpet that matched the walls, painted brown with a pinch of red, the color of my emotions and thoughts.

"Hey," yelled someone from the entrance of the salon. I walked back toward the salon area where Jeff had entered carrying a box of supplies.

"Hey, Juan," he yelled. "Where am I setting up?"

I walked over to the third chair. "You can set up here," I said, glancing over at Rob shaking his head from left to right. Jeff walked over to the chair and began to set his things down. I tried my best to hear what Rob was saying. I read his lips.

"Don't sit that faggot next to me. I don't like him." Rob's nostrils were swollen as he pointed at the fifth chair.

"You know what? Better yet, you can take the fifth chair," I said to Jeff. Jeff was brown-skinned and skinny as ever with long black hair. If this wasn't planet earth and we weren't humans, then his face could easily be mistaken for a dinosaur. Wearing a pair of dirty-washed jeans, a tight T-shirt and Converses he briskly rushed past me to his station. I walked over to the stereo that sat on the floor by the water cooler and turned it on. Then I walked over to Rob who seemed frustrated now that Jeff had made his arrival.

"What's wrong with you?" I whispered to Rob, trying not to let Jeff hear us.

"I don't like *her*," he said, still shaking his head.

"What you mean, you don't like her? I mean him. Do you even know him?" I asked.

"No, not really. But do you remember when Jason Revlon threw that ball in New York last spring?"

"Mmm-hmm," I said, shaking my head.

"And remember when that fight broke out between my cousin BJ and that faggot named Marcus?"

"I guess I remember," I responded.

"Well, that little bitch over there jumped in the fight and they rolled on my cousin BJ. When I get the chance I'ma tear his ass up."

"Look, Rob, please don't start anything in my shop," I pleaded.

"No, I'm not gonna do anything in here but just know that I'ma get him when the time is right," Rob continued.

I let out a big sigh and placed my hand on my forehead when twin sisters Keisha and Kya walked in. I call them "Day" and "Night" because, although they are twins, they aren't identical. Keisha is the sexy chocolate one and Kya is more on the light-skinned side. Both are skinny and they were both wearing micro-braids.

"Hey, y'all," said Kya, walking over to me and giving me a hug with Keisha following right behind her.

"Hey, I'm loving the matching sweats," I said to the both of them, referring to their pink sweat suits.

"Thanks," they said in unison.

"Where do we set up?" Keisha asked as I pointed them to their chairs that separated them between Jeff and Rob. They walked over to their stations when my first client came through the door.

"Do you have an appointment?" I asked the brown-skinned girl who seemed to be no more than eighteen.

"Yes, I made an appointment with Jeff," she said. I pointed

her in the direction of Jeff's chair. She sashayed over to the chair and took a seat when the front door opened again but this time it wasn't a customer.

The wind chimes that hung above the door made a jingling sound as he walked in. Alicia Keys' "My Boo" filled my ears with great emotion as my mouth watered from this slice of fantasy that stood before me. He wore a pair of Rocawear capri pants with the hanging strings exposing his brown-skinned hairy legs that led to his silky, caramel-colored ankles. Gracing his feet were a pair of fresh white Air Force Ones.

I looked up at his face to see his flawless skin with a nice thick mustache that formed a goatee. His braided cornrows flowed down the back of his neck like butter. He also sported a white wife beater that complemented his toned and broad shoulders that showed off muscle-bound veins in his arms.

Shorty was getting looks from Rob, Keisha, Kya, Jeff, and the eighteen-year-old who sat in Jeff's chair. He licked his lips very proper like L.L. would. Just seeing him walk his way into the shop that I owned fired up that thing in between my legs.

"Ayo, wassup, girl," he said to Keisha as he continued to walk toward the back area where I stood. "Which one of you owns this shop?" he asked, looking around.

I spoke up immediately. "I do. Why? Wassup?" I asked, trying to talk his language. That *thug* style.

"Ayo, wassup, playa? I wanted to know if I could interest you in some DVDs," he said, pointing toward the direction of the door. During the course of this time about three more people walked in with appointments.

"Well, what kind of DVDs do you have?" I asked simply to start something. I knew damn well I really didn't want to buy no damn DVDs. I don't even watch TV like that.

"I have *Hustle & Flow*, *Beauty Shop* and a lot others. Come outside and take a look." He walked over to the door and opened it. I followed as Ieshia rushed in.

"Hey, Juan, where are you going?" she asked, staring at me through her dark shades.

"I'm going outside to see what DVDs he has. I'll be right back." I went outside and closed the door behind me. The spring air felt mellow as a wash of comfort came over my body. Walking him to his car made me feel at ease as the warm wind blew against my face. We came upon a green Ford Expedition. He popped the back door and opened it to find boxes full of DVDs and CDs.

"See, whatever you want, I got it," he said, grabbing a handful of DVDs and showing them to me. I looked back at the shop to see Rob and Ieshia gazing through the front window smiling.

"Damn, your peeps staring at me n' shit. Wassup with that? What they think, I'm gonna kidnap you or sumthin'?" he asked, sounding annoyed. I stood there trying not to let him know that I was digging him. "Yo, check it. I don't like the way they keep lookin' at me so here's what I'ma do." He placed the DVDs back into the box and closed the door. He went around to the passenger's seat and grabbed a pen and a piece of paper and began to scribble.

"Shit, this pen don't work," he said, throwing the pen into the street and reaching back into the truck to get another one. I admired his biceps as he flexed his muscles, scrambling around in the console for another pen. After rearranging a few items in the console he found a black pen and began writing on the piece of paper.

"Here, take my cell number and give me a call lata. I'ma come bring the DVDs to you without all those kats around, aiight," he said, handing me the paper. I grabbed it and stuck it in my back pocket as he ran around to the driver's side and hopped in.

I began walking back to the shop when he called out to me.

"Yo," he hollered as I turned around to face him, blocking the sun from my eyes with my hand. "Don't forget, shawty," he said as he winked at me, then turned his system up high, blasting Peedi Crakk's song "Gotta Have It," and sped off. My heart melted instantly. I stood there for a moment reminiscing about how Darnell used to give me that same feeling. I thought, *he didn't even tell me his name. Does he even know mine? I'm not even gonna call him. I don't want any DVDs really.* I reached down into my back pocket and pull the paper out. Sure it was written B-R-Y-A-N-T. I smiled, thinking of the fact that I had the option of calling him even though I didn't think I would.

$$\$\$\$\$\$$$

Tiredness overwhelmed my mind and my body. Today had been a very successful day at Ché Mystic. I had grossed about a thousand dollars alone so I was straight. Not to mention that I still had about $175,000 put aside in the bank for a rainy day.

I relaxed in the recliner that sat in the plush family room of my apartment. I leaned back on the headrest and let my mind run and exhale all the stress that had been brought upon me. My heart felt heavy once again as I continued to lie there and think about the man whom I once loved and who once loved me. I turned to look out the window at the night sky and watched every star twinkle in the distance. I closed my eyes to thank God for His many blessings and to ask Him again why did He have to take Darnell away from me.

My eyes began to water as I let a lonely tear run down my face. I could feel how sad I had become the day he'd left this earth. I felt depressed and not to the point where I needed to kill myself but to where I needed to live in this world alone. Through all my shame and guilt that I carried around with me for letting him die there in that bank alone, I needed something or someone to help me relax and stimulate my mind; not physically but mentally as well. Someone to stimulate me to the point of no return. Maybe I do need to start watching TV more often.

Then I remembered Bryant's phone number was still in my pants pocket. As I continued to sit I thought about how he'd left such an impression on me today. I got the number from my pocket and called him. I let the phone ring at least three times before he picked up.

"Yerp," he greeted in a deep sexy voice.

"Hello, can I speak with Bryant, please?" I asked in a shaken voice. The nervousness sat so deep down in my soul that my underarms were starting to sweat.

"Who dis?"

"Ah, this is Juan. You came into my salon today. You were talkin' to me about some DVDs that you were selling."

"Oh yeah, the lil' pretty dude. Wassup?" he asked as I almost swallowed my spit from what he'd said. He labeled me as the "pretty dude." A smile immediately came across my face.

"Yeah, my name is Juan," I said.

"Oh, excuse me, Mr. Juan. My bad if I offended you."

"Oh, no, not at all. You didn't offend me. I was just caught off guard," I rebutted.

"Caught off guard, huh? Why? 'Cuz I said you was pretty?"

I was speechless.

"Naw. I didn't think you looked at me that way, that's all," I said with my hands shaking.

"Oh okay, well, I call 'em as I see 'em, that's all." Once again he brought a smile to my face. "Listen, what are you doing now?"

"Well, right now, I'm not doing anything. Are you coming to my crib to show me the DVDs?"

"Yeah, I can do that. But first I have to get me sumthin' to eat. I'm hungrier than a muthafucka."

There was dead silence on the phone. I didn't know what to say so I said the first thing that came to mind. "Well, I can make sumthin' to eat and have it ready by the time you get here." *What am I saying? He gonna think that I'm some type of fag or sumthin'.*

"Yeah, that's cool. What are you cooking?"

"I can whip up a pot of spaghetti, if that's cool with you," I said, still shaking nervously with the phone in my hand.

"Aiight, bet. You must really know how to throw down in the kitchen, huh?" he said, laughing.

"I do aiight. I ain't no Betty Crocker or nuffin' like that," I responded.

"Aiight, well, do this. Give me ya address and I'll be there in like an hour. I gotta go handle sumthin' real quick."

I quickly gave him my address and told him to have the lady downstairs buzz me when he arrived. I threw the phone on the couch and rushed into the kitchen to find a pot to boil some water. It wasn't enough time to thaw out the ground beef so I jumped in my car and hurried down the street to the super-market. *Am I going out of my mind?*

I was sitting there in my living room feeling sorry for myself and now I was about to fix a nigga who I don't even know something to eat. What state of mind was I in to be giving him my address and telling him I would cook for him? For all I knew he could be a mass murderer. *Juan, you just need to think. Take a minute and think.*

The gun that was placed under my bed some time ago by Darnell was still there if I had any problems. My building was very secure if someone were to come and try to kill me. With all that at hand I figured I should be cool.

While I let the noodles simmer on the stove I quickly jumped in the shower and put on some sweet-smelling oil to have the mood set by the time he arrived. Instead of wearing my usual jeans and fitted shirt I replaced the outfit that I had on earlier with a pair of black Rocawear velour sweats, a wife beater and a pair of Nike sweat socks with matching Nike flip-flops. I put my hair back into a ponytail held by a rubber band instead of a Scrunchie.

Within a half-hour my creation of a meal of spaghetti was done. I turned the radio on and popped in Mariah Carey's new CD and let number two play. As "We Belong Together" filled the air I poured a glass of wine to help relax my anxious mind. I sat down on the couch and listened to the entire CD. I must have dozed off for a minute because the next thing I knew the CD was not playing and the hour that Bryant had told me he'd be here had turned into three.

I looked up at the huge clock that hung on the living room wall and it read a quarter to one in the morning. I palmed my face in my hands thinking how naïve I could have been about this boy. I was acting like a high school girl that has a crush on someone from the football team. The buzz from the speaker on the wall startled me. I got up and walked over and pressed the "talk" button.

"Yes," I said, letting the button go and waiting for a response.

"Mr. Jiles, a gentleman by the name of Bryant Thompson is here to see you," responded the Asian female voice on the other end.

"Thanks, Trudy. You can send him up." After giving her the orders I ran into the bathroom to find the toothbrush and toothpaste to brush away any odors that formulated in my mouth while I was asleep. I brushed heavily and spit out the excess water into the bowl when the doorbell rang. I wiped my mouth and looked at myself in the mirror one last time before heading down the hallway to the door.

I unlocked the door and there Bryant stood wearing the same gear that he'd had on earlier. His eyelids hung low as if he was super high.

"Wassup, shawty," he said, walking in, taking my hand and balling it up and letting our shoulders touch. "My bad for being late. I'm hungry as shit. Where's the grub?" he asked, walking into my apartment and looking around.

"It's in the kitchen, I have to heat it up," I answered.

"Damn, this crib is bangin'. You live here by yourself or does your bitch live here too?" He continued to walk throughout the living room while grabbing his crotch.

"Naw, I live alone," I said, yelling from in the kitchen while turning on the stove.

"Oh, aiight, dat's wassup. Can I sit down?" He pointed to the loveseat.

"Sure, go ahead. Did you bring the DVDs?"

"Shit, I forgot them. They in the car, I'ma get 'em after I eat 'cuz a nigga is starving."

I fixed him a big plate of spaghetti with the sauce deliciously towering over the noodles. He came to the kitchen table and sat down and we began to eat. I watched his every move as he slurped each noodle in his mouth. This nigga was turning me on.

"Would you like something to drink?" I asked, getting up and opening the refrigerator.

"Sure, what you got?" he asked, lifting his head from his plate and placing his eyes on the way my ass stood out in these sweats.

"What you want?" I asked seductively. He then turned from me and back down to his plate.

"Just grip me a soda," he said as I reached up to the cabinet to get a glass to pour him some grape soda.

"Ayo, call some bitches," he said out of nowhere. I was completely caught off guard as I tried to respond the best as I could.

"Who do you want me to call?" I said, sitting back down at the table and eating my food.

"Just call some bitches, do you know any?" he asked almost finishing his food.

"Naw," I responded.

"How a pretty muthafucka like you don't know any bitches?" He paused for a minute waiting for the answer. I thought quickly.

"All the bitches I know of have boyfriends."

"Oh aiight." We both finished our plates. He then got up and ran down to the parking lot to retrieve some DVDs while I loaded the dishwasher and cleaned the kitchen.

By the time he came back I was done my duties in the kitchen and was ready to relax on the couch. He came through the door with only one movie in hand.

"Yo, have you seen Tyler Perry's *Diary of a Mad Black Woman* yet?" he asked, walking toward me with the movie.

"Naw, I saw the play but not the movie."

"Yo, this shit is funny. Here, put it in," he said, handing me the movie. I got up and walked over to the entertainment center where I placed the DVD in the machine. He sat back on the love seat.

"Yo, you got an ashtray?" He pulled a bag of weed from his pocket along with a Philly Dutch. I went into the kitchen to get an astray from the cabinet. I normally kept them for when Anthony came over because I didn't smoke. I handed him the ashtray as he began to roll himself a fatty.

By the time he lit the Dutch, the movie was just beginning. I watched as Kimberly Elise acted as stupid as she looked when she was being cheated on by that ugly-ass black man. The least Tyler Perry could do is have a cute man to play the part of her husband.

"Here," he said, handing me the Dutch with swollen cheeks. I didn't know whether I should take it or turn it down. Then I thought of my life and how it never seems like I do much of anything to have fun. I took the Dutch.

I inhaled it and swallowed the smoke like Darnell had taught me. I exhaled, then inhaled again. This time I gave it a long pull. I felt the smoke clouding my mind as I began to cough a bit.

"That shit is good, ain't it?" He reached out for me to pass it back to him. I passed the Dutch as I tried to get my focus back to the movie. Out of the corner of my eyes I noticed him un-buckling his belt. I looked over to him with a confused look.

"What are you about to do?" I asked as he continued to blow smoke circles into the air.

"I'ma finish smoking this Dutch while I get my dick sucked. That's what I'm about to do," he replied. "Now come over here and head-sprung this shit, nigga." I got up, walked over to him, dropped to my knees and did as I was told.

VI
DICKNOTIZED

"Yeah, that's it. Do what you do," said Bryant as I dropped to my knees. After unbuckling his belt buckle he unzipped his pants. I saw his hard dick ready to explode from his white-and-navy-blue boxers. I grabbed his pulsating rod and rubbed it back and forth looking up at his face as he continued to blow smoke circles.

He leaned back into the love seat still putting the Dutch to his lips. I released his throbbing muscle through the slit of his boxers and began to taste it with my tongue.

I massaged his mushroom head between my tongue and the roof of my mouth. He tasted so good to me. The lighted reflection from the television bounced from the walls as the movie continued to play. Still taking pulls with one hand, he grabbed the top of my head with the other pushing me down onto his chocolate nine inches. He placed the Dutch into the ashtray before he palmed my head with both hands pumping himself harder and harder into my mouth.

The hanging saliva along with his pre-cum escaped the sides of my mouth dripping down onto his shaft and falling directly on his pubic hairs.

"Damn, dude, that shit feels so good." He let out a huge sigh. My jaws began to tense as he started to pump faster. I began to gag from the force of him gagging me with his pole. "That shit is proper," he said with his eyes closed as he leaned his head back against the couch.

After a few more pumps deep into my mouth he let out the biggest explosion down my throat. Without stopping I continued to suck his strawberry cream until it was deep into my belly. I licked his dick bone dry.

"Yeah, that's what I'm talkin' about," he said, sticking his dick back into his boxers and reaching over to the ashtray to re-light his Dutch. As he lit it I grabbed his arm and placed it around my body as we both sat on the love seat and continued to watch the movie.

$$$$$$$

"For real?" asked Anthony with excited eyes as we sat at an outdoor restaurant table on the curb of South Street. I was just finishing up my stack of Buffalo wings when I began telling him about my sexual night.

"You have got to be kidding me. What made him do that?" he asked, filling his mouth with garden salad.

"I guess, 'cuz he knew I looked good. I knew he wanted me from the jump," I said feeling very vain as I began to lick my fingers.

"Bitch, you better work. Does he have a girlfriend? Or I boy-friend, should I say?"

"Not that I know of. If he does, he didn't act like it. After I sucked his dick we watched a movie and then from there it moved into the bedroom and bitch, trust me when I tell you. *He broke my BACK,*" I continued to explain as we both started to laugh.

"Oh shit," he said, trying not to spit out his food. "How big is he?"

"He's about an eight or a nine. Shit, maybe nine and a half. Bitch, it's not like I had a ruler handy."

"Well, can he work it?"

"Can he?" I said as my eyes widened. "That nigga almost knocked my tooth loose," I responded.

"Now see that's what I need," said Anthony. "Someone that can bring it like it needs to be brought." Anthony stopped and took a sip of his pink lemonade.

"Are you going to your hair show tonight?"

"Yeah, I guess so. Would you like to come along?" I asked him as I gripped my glass and took a sip of Merlot.

"I guess so. I don't have shit else to do. Darrell is in the streets as always," he said.

I set my glass down on the table as a mob of people filled the streets on this lovely spring day.

"Whatever happened to that dude Reggie that you introduced me to?" I asked.

"Man, he was corny as hell. And he was dirty. How you gonna have a professional basketball player in your family and dress dirty?" he said, talking with his hands. We both laughed.

"Well, I'll go to the hair show for a little while but then Bryant's supposed to be stopping through again," I said, raising my arm above my head and snapping my fingers.

"Okay, then let's go. Check, please," Anthony said, waving toward the waiter to get his attention. He paid for both of our meals and we left the restaurant. We walked along South Street with my soul feeling *good.* That's just what I needed: some good sex to help me get through my life. As we walked into the RBK store my cell phone rang. It was Bryant.

"Hello," I said.

"Wassup, Shawty?" he asked in his ever-so-sexy voice. My heart melted hotter than vanilla ice cream in an oven. I then became dreamy-eyed and all I could do was block out everyone around me and focus on him.

"Hey, Bryant. How are you?" I asked, walking over to the curb to let the other people pass while Anthony proceeded to walk into the store.

"I'm aiight, what you up to?" he asked.

"I chillin' out with my boy. We're at South Street."

"Oh, you at South Street, huh? You gonna pick me up sumthin'?" he asked as I held the phone tightly to my ear.

"Sure, what do you want?"

"Just grip me a pair of sneeks. Some Jordans, na'mean?" I was flattered that he had asked *me* to buy him sumthin'. I was really feeling the love that came from him.

"Okay, Bryant. What size do you wear?" I asked, smiling.

"You can grip me a ten and a half." I could tell he was smoking something. I could hear him blow through the phone.

"I got you. Will I be seeing you this evening?" I asked excitedly.

"Yeah, I'ma come through like around twelve, aiight, shawty?"

"Okay."

"Aiight, I'll holla."

"Okay."

"One." Then the line went dead. I closed my cell phone and walked into the store where Anthony was. The sounds of Lil' Kim's "No Time" filled the store as there employees rushing around trying to get their customers situated and wall-to-wall cuties. The store was mixed with all types of races from blacks, whites, Chinese thugs holding tight to their Chinese girlfriends, and then there was Anthony and me.

I walked straight to the back where Anthony stood checking out a shoe. He stood there with his hands on his hips.

"These niggas can't take me," he said, trying to get someone's attention who could help him.

"What's wrong?" I asked him as I noticed his face starting to get a little red.

"Excuse me. Can I get some help," he hissed at the young Asian man who seemed to be out of breath. He came over to us.

"Can you get me this in a seven?" Anthony gave him the shoe.

"What's wrong?" I asked again taking a seat on the bench.

"Some dude called me a faggot," he said, now annoyed.

"Who?"

"That nigga over there." He nodded his head in the direction of four teenage males. None looked older than eighteen. When I turned my head to view them, they all were leaving the store.

"Don't worry about them," I said. "They're probably some young broke-ass ghetto kids," I continued. The Asian guy returned with Anthony's shoe.

"Do you need to try this on?" he said, taking the shoe out of the box.

"No, I already know it fits. Thanks." Anthony grabbed the box from the guy and walked to the cashier.

"Are you okay?" I asked, following him in tow.

"This shit pisses me the fuck off." He pulled out his money to pay for the shoes when the thought popped in my mind that I needed to pick up Bryant a pair of Jordans.

"We have to go down to Foot Locker 'cause Bryant wants me to get him a pair of Jordans," I said proudly.

"Damn, didn't you meet him yesterday?" he said, putting his change from his shoes into his man bag.

"Yeah, so what."

"Why is he asking you for shit? He doesn't even know you."

"We know each other pretty well, I might say," I bragged.

"Well, you know what they say…"

"What?"

"You shouldn't buy your lover shoes cuz he'll walk out of your life," he said, grabbing his bag from the counter. I giggled and we walked toward the door. I looked down at the floor and began smiling, thinking how last night was a perfect evening and how I couldn't wait until later tonight.

With Anthony leading the path we walked out of the store and onto the street. Two teenage boys ran over quickly to us and began waling on Anthony with balled-up fists. I began to scream as the other two boys ran toward me. I quickly threw up my guard as fast as I could before they began punching me in my face and stomach.

I managed to free myself, only to see Anthony lying on the ground and the other two boys kicking him non-stop. People began to crowd the scene in front of the sneaker store as all four boys scattered. I held my face to stop the pain as I kneeled down to Anthony's body. His head lay pressed against the concrete.

"Somebody call an ambulance," I yelled with tears welling in my eyes. People continued to stand around speechless and motionless.

"Anthony," I yelled. I didn't really want to move him but I did want to check to see if his heart was beating. The crowd began to grow as I heard police sirens in the distance. The wind began to blow as Anthony's body shivered. I rapidly took my jacket off to cover his body. In minutes the paramedics bombarded their way through the crowd.

I stood up and out of the way so the medics could do their job. They worked on him for about five minutes before placing a brace on his neck and positioning him on the stretcher.

"Are you with him, sir?" the Caucasian man asked who helped to place him in the ambulance.

"Yes, I am," I said, grabbing Anthony's belongings and hopping in the back of the van.

After about two and a half hours at the hospital and after I had been examined I was allowed to go in and see Anthony. Doctors said Anthony was lucky considering the type of beating he had suffered. God had given my friend a second chance at life. He had suffered a broken rib cage, a broken jaw, and a dislocated shoulder with a few minor cuts and bruises.

I walked into the room where Anthony lay asleep. I said a silent prayer to God thanking Him for sparing Anthony's life. He was the only family I had. I walked over to him and kissed him on the cheek. I would be back to visit him first thing in the morning.

$$$$$

It was half past one when Trudy buzzed the intercom to tell me that Bryant was downstairs. I told her to send him up.

Being as though I was officially seeing him now, there was no need for me to be fully dressed. I met him at the door wearing nothing but a T-shirt and a pair of boxers. He walked in wearing a gray-and-black sweat suit and carrying flowers.

"Hey, Bryant," I said with a semi-smile.

"Hey, Baby. These are for you." He handed me the bouquet of fresh cut roses and calla lilies.

"Aww, Bryant, thank you," I said, reaching up and planting a kiss on his soft lips. He walked in and sat down in the dimly lit living room. I went into the kitchen to put the flowers in a vase of water, with him following behind. The light in the kitchen was much brighter than the light in the living room. I knew it was only a matter of time before he saw my face so I sat the flowers down on the counter. I quickly turned around to get the questioning over.

"Damn, Baby, what happened?" he said, examining my jaw.

My eyes began to fill up with tears again. "Me and my friend Anthony got into a fight today down South Street," I explained. I looked down at the floor and then back at his face.

"Shit. Are you okay?" He grabbed both of my arms and stared directly into my eyes. I tried to hold back my tears but I couldn't.

"I'll be okay, but my friend is hurt badly," I confessed while sobbing hysterically. He grabbed me with both of his arms and pulled me toward him. The weed smell from his breath was replaced by the scent of his cologne. I grabbed his back and held him close as tightly as I could while letting my tears flow.

"J.J., it's gonna be okay, I promise you," he said as he continued to hold me. I felt so calm while in his arms. I trusted every word he said as I held him tighter.

"I'm glad that you're here," I said, letting him go and standing back so I could look in his eyes. I never remembered seeing a pair of eyes so beautiful. This man looked like an older model of Lil' Bow Wow.

"Are you sure that your jaw doesn't hurt, Baby?" he asked.

I put my hand gently over my face. "Yeah, it hurts a little bit but I'll be okay," I responded and wiped my eyes.

"Naw, Baby, I got something that will help take that pain away. Do the police know who did this?" he asked, turning around and walking back into the living room.

"No, they don't. I don't think they even looked, to tell you the truth." I turned around to the flowers when I heard the front door slam. I ran to the door. "Where are you going?" I yelled down the hall as he stood in front of the elevator.

"I'm going to the car to get my stuff. I'll be right back, J.J. Go inside; I'll make you some tea when I come back up." The elevator bell rang and he stepped on. I tried to smile but the pain on my swollen face was intense. I ran inside and proceeded to put my beautiful flowers in water. I couldn't find a vase that was big enough to hold the flowers so I placed them on the counter. *I could use these flowers to take to the hospital in the morning. I know Ant sure could use some cheering up.*

"Ayo, J, I'm back," Bryant announced closing the door behind him. I went into the living room and sat down on the couch.

"Yo, get the ashtray," he said, positioning himself on the couch next to where I sat. I went into the kitchen and brought back the ashtray and sat it down in front of us. I then went over to the stereo to turn on some music. *Maybe a little Will Downing will help complete the mood,* I thought as I placed the CD into the tray. I went back to Bryant where he was splitting the Dutch open. I watched him as he disregarded all of the blunt contents and replaced it with his killer weed. I prepared myself for the relaxation that Bryant had brought to me. As the events of today played over and over in my mind, Bryant's stimulation as well as our passionate night of lovemaking quickly replaced my thoughts.

I continued to sit there as he prepared our relaxation, but before he closed up the Dutch he gently poured a few clumps of white substance throughout the grain of the blunt. Afterward he neatly patched up the Dutch and burnt it so that it would hold. He lit that muthafucka and we cruised, and with each puff, I was enjoying the ride.

I placed my hands down by my side as Bryant placed the blunt in between my lips. I then inhaled softly as I let the electric relaxation take over my mind. I leaned back on the couch watching him take a few puffs. All of a sudden he looked ten times better than he would normally look. I became erect instantly as he passed the Dutch back over to me. I grabbed my hard-on to let him know that it was on and poppin'. My dick extended through my boxers as he smiled. *He knows what time it is.*

I got up and walked in the direction toward my bedroom. It felt as if I was floating on a cloud. The furniture seemed smaller than its normal size and the hallway leading to my bedroom seemed longer than normal. I anxiously walked into my bedroom with Bryant following behind. I stumbled a little because I thought there were steps leading from the hallway to the bedroom.

"Are you okay there?" he asked, trying to help me regain my balance.

"Yeah, I'm fine. Let me get another pull," I demanded as I fell onto the bed with him falling right on top of me. I needed to do a double-take because for a minute I thought he was Darnell. I could smell his presence.

"C'mon, J.J., you gon' make me drop it," he said, putting the blunt in between my lips. I took a long pull as I let the smoke sit in my mouth for a hot second before I exhaled.

I knew that Bryant was exactly what I needed because all of a sudden the pain in my face was gone. He'd given me exactly what the doctor had ordered. He took a long pull of the blunt and placed his lips against mine as we performed the *shotgun.*

I could not let his lips go. As we began kissing our tongues seemed like they had a mind of their own as they began to wrestle. I gripped him around his neck and pulled him in closer to me as he tried to drop the Dutch in the ashtray that sat on the nightstand.

"Damn, Baby, you missed me that much?" he asked, continuously kissing me non-stop. I could feel his "Daddy dick" poking me through his sweats. I grabbed it and I could feel the blood rushing through the veins as he made his dick jump continuously.

He began to kiss me on my neck and started to work his way down to my nipples. I made an exotic moan to let him know that whatever he wanted to do I was willing. He licked over my entire chest and worked his tongue down my torso. He made his way to the top of my boxers as my dick stood brick.

"Now that's what I'm talkin' 'bout," he said erotically as he yanked the top of my underwear. He pulled my boxers down slowly licking his way through my angel hairs. My body felt limp on the bed through complete darkness. He stood up and commenced to removing his shirt. Then he went back to what he was doing. He played with the head of my dick with his tongue. I could feel my nut ejaculating prematurely as he slurped every drop.

Then he downed me like a Popsicle on a summer's day. His mouth grew wider and wider as he deep throated my manhood. I grabbed the back of his head and pumped my thug into his mouth. He worked my meat like a pro. After he was done servicing my dick, he began to suck on my balls. I sighed heavily as I watched the room spin in different directions. I rubbed his braids back and forth, watching him go to work.

This is my bitch, I thought to myself as I pumped my eight inches into his brain. He then pulled back up to catch his breath. We both laughed. *Oh fa' real*, I thought. This nigga didn't know what he was getting himself into. He jumped up and stripped down completely before jumping back on the bed and climbing on top of me. He pulled my boxers the rest of the way off and tossed them onto the floor. He gripped the side of my neck with his teeth as he sucked hard, raising my legs above my head and ramming his dick into me.

"Aaahhhh," I yelled from the pain. I grabbed his shoulders and held tight as he pumped harder in my ass.

"Damn, this shit feels good, J," he whispered into my ear. I let my body go onto his and relaxed as he put me to work.

"C'mon, work that shit, boy," he yelled. I started to groan louder. I could feel him banging into my spine. He pumped faster and harder. I sucked on my index finger and made it as wet as I could before I passionately entered his back door. My finger began to rise through his anus when I decided my other finger would join in. The deeper I went into him the deeper he went into me.

"Go 'head, boy. Go deeper," he said. By then my fingers were all the way in. I couldn't go anymore.

"Make a nigga nut," he said continuously to pump harder. "What's my name?"

"Bryant," I whispered. He moved his torso faster and then in circles.

"What's my name?" He yearned louder. I grabbed the back of his head and held tighter. The fluids started to shoot from my dick as I willingly let him take over my body. "Bryant," I yelled again with my body trembling from the smash I had busted.

"C'mon, boy, what is my muthafuckin' name?" he repeatedly said while pumping faster.

"*Daddy Dick,*" I yelled for the last time as he shot all his man juice inside my body.

"Damn, Baby. That's good," he said, sucking in my lips with his tongue. His body lay pressed against mine with love juice sandwiched between. I kissed his sweaty forehead. *Thank you*, I thought. We continued to lie on the bed as he fell asleep in my arms without removing himself. I listened to his loud snores as I thought about what had happened today. Hmm, today wasn't such a bad day after all.

$$\$\$\$\$\$\$$$

The music was bumping as I shook my head to the beat of Nicole Wray's "Make it Hot." I was busy doing a sewn-in weave on one my regulars when Bryant entered the shop followed by one of his boys.

"Wassup, peoples," said Bryant as he held the door for his bull to carry in the box of DVDs.

"We got CDs and DVDs," announced Bryant, walking past my chair as if he didn't know me. I tried my hardest not to stare to make our relationship known. He walked around sucking a cherry lollipop and wearing an oversized white tee, a pair of Miskeen capris and a pair of Prada sneakers with ankle socks. Tailing behind him was a light-skinned young bull that had to be no older than eighteen with sandy-brown hair and basically sporting the same gear as Bryant. As the young bull sat the box down on the floor Bryant went over to holla at Kya.

"Wassup, cutie?" he said, licking his lips and twirling the lollipop in and out of his mouth. Kya, who sported a long weave with Chinese bangs, a tight wife beater that read *Princess* across the chest and a pair of booty shorts, stopped what she was doing and gave Bryant the time of day.

"Nothing," she said in a shy tone.

"I'm sayin', shawty, you gotta man?" asked Bryant as if he had some intentions of getting with her. *Does he not see me standing here?*

"Actually I don't," she responded. I was getting heated. I couldn't believe that he would do this shit in front of my face.

"Um, there's no soliciting in the shop, fellas. Could you please leave?" I demanded, trying to be smart. Bryant looked at me with a smart-aleck look.

"Oh my bad, we gon' leave." He turned to the young bull. "Ayo, take that box out to the truck," he instructed. And the young bull did as he was told.

"What's ya numba, shawty?" Bryant asked, pulling out his cell phone and punching in Kya's number. I could sense that Rob could see the fire in my eyes but he, Keisha, and Jeff all had their eyes on Bryant.

"Aiight, I'ma call you lata," Bryant said. He closed his cell phone and gave me one last look before leaving the shop. By the time Bryant left, Nicole's song had gone off and B2K was starting to play.

"Girl, he was the bomb. You better not sleep on that, Kya," screamed Rob as soon as the door shut behind Bryant.

"Huh, you think I am? Oh, no, I need a man. And boy was he fine," she responded. "I can't wait to get a taste of that," he added.

"Girl, I wish I could be a fly on the wall," teased Rob.

"Excuse me for a minute. I have to make an important phone call," I said to my client as I placed my comb down on my station and walked quickly into my office and closed the door.

I decided to use my cell phone and not the shop's phone in case someone was to pick up the cordless.

"Yo," Bryant said after the first ring. I know he could tell that I was heated.

"What the fuck do you take me for, a fool?" I snapped.

"J.J., what are you talkin' about?

"How you gonna come up in *my* salon and disrespect me that way?"

"C'mon, man, you wouldn't let me grind. You know I need to make some money to feed my seed. Why did you put us out?" he shot back.

"No, I put you out after you tried to holla at Kya," I spat.

"C'mon now, J, you should know me better than that. It was all game. I can't let muthafuckas think I'm comin' in here to see a dude. You gon' have to cease with that jealous shit, man, for real, if you wanna be with me." The phone was silent for a minute.

"Well, do you have plans on ever calling her?" I asked.

"Fuck no. Look, I told you. It was game."

"Alright, I hear you," I said, trying not to sound stupid.

"Now, is that all you want? I got work to do."

"Yeah, that's all I wanted."

"Aiight, one."

$$$$$

The bell rang to let me off the elevator on the fifth floor of Pennsylvania Memorial Hospital. I checked in with the female security officer at the desk to direct me to Anthony's room. I wondered if any of his family members had come to see him. Probably not because his mother had abandoned him at a very young age, due to his sexual orientation. It's sad because it seems that gay people as a whole will always get the shaft. I walked down the hall to room 532.

"Hello," I said, knocking and opening the door at the same time. The TV played on mute and Anthony lay in the bed on his side.

"Hey there." I walked over to him and planted a kiss on his forehead. I put the flowers down on the table that sat close to his bed. "Look what I brought. How are you feeling?"

He stared at me as he pointed to the tube that hung from his nose. I realized he couldn't talk but he tried to formulate words with his dry, chapped lips.

"No, don't try to talk and try not to move a lot." I grabbed his hand.

"Everything's gonna be okay," I explained with watery eyes. I reached for a tissue to dab his tears.

"Now I didn't come here for us to cry. I came here to visit and buss it up with you all day." He looked at me, trying to crack a smile as his eyes lit up. "Yes, that's right, *all day*. This morning I gave Rob his own set of keys and made him manager. He will be calling the shots at Ché Mystic and he will be closing." I rubbed my hand down the sides of his face. "I'm here, so don't you worry," I assured him. I pulled up a chair but before I sat down, I went over to the window to open the curtains to let a bit of sunlight in. I then sat down at his bedside.

"Now, what are you watching?" I said, looking up at the TV where an episode of Montell Williams was on. I looked down to see Anthony's hand across mine. I looked at his eyes and figured he was trying to tell me something.

"What's wrong?" I asked. He put his hands into a talking position. "Are you in pain?" He shook his head no. "Well what's wrong then?" I asked again. He put his hands in a talking position again.

"You wanna talk?" He moved his head up and down. "About what? What happened yesterday?" He shook his head no. "Your family?" No clue. "Me?" Then it hit bingo. "What about me?"

He gave me the face as to say, *it's obvious.* "Bryant?" He made the facial expression to say *I hit the nail on the head.*

I began conversing with him using a notepad with me writing things down for him. The nurse came in once or twice to check on him and his vital signs. In between nursing checks I stepped out the room to give Bryant a call.

"Hey, Bry," I greeted.

"J.J., wassup?"

"Nothing much, missing you." I smiled. It seemed as if there was a lot of noise in the background. "Where are you?"

"I'm out chillin' with my shawty, you know, doin' what I do," he said. "Yo, dat shit that you asked me for...," he said, changing the subject.

"Yeah..."

"I'ma need about three G's to get it for you, aiight. Do you have that?"

"Yeah, I have to go to the bank and get it," I responded.

"Aiight, you do that and I'ma get at you lata, aiight?"

"Alright, Bryant, but who..." I tried to get out my sentence but before I could the line went dead. I know I needed to pace myself because I was jumping the gun. *Maybe he's just talkin' bout an old friend. I know he's not out with another girl because he wouldn't do that shit to me. Well, what I'll do is calm down and go back in the room and tend to Anthony. He needs my help right now and I'm not gonna worry about no bullshit until later.*

During lunch I'll run over to the bank and get the money he needs, I thought. *Then we're gonna have a lovely time tonight, just me and him getting' our freak on. I'll sit back and let him do what he does to make me comfortable, like he did last night. Man, if it only takes three G's for him to make me feel like he did last night, it is well worth it.*

VII
Baby Mama Madness

The room was dark as I lay in the middle of the bed as the room spun. The tears in my eyes rolled down my cheeks as I thought about my younger years. The beatings, the scalding, and the molestation. *Does my father have any idea of the trauma he put me through?* I loved him, I trusted him. *How could he do this to me? How could God allow this to happen to me?* I was always a good boy growing up. I always got good grades in school. *What in the hell was wrong with me?*

I got up and walked into the kitchen for a drink to calm me down. I decided not to get a glass to be classy; instead I went straight for the bottle. Tanqueray straight, that's what I was in the mood for. I went back into the bathroom with swollen eyes and looked into the mirror.

"A poor excuse for a man," I said to myself as the tears mixed with my snot ran down my face. I banged my fist on the wall. *How did I end up like this? How did I end up like this?* I took another swig of the bottle, then raced into the bedroom to get the cordless phone from its base. The clock read one-thirty and Bryant was not here yet. He met me at four o' clock to get my money and the bastard wasn't here. *I'm tired of calling him; he's not gonna answer his cell phone.* I quickly thought of Rob's phone number and dialed it.

"Hello," Rob answered, sounding asleep.

"Yeah, Rob, hey it's me, Juan," I said, trying not to sound like I'd been crying.

"Yeah, Juan, what's up?"

"I need the phone number to your boy, you know the one that you be getting your shit from. I need his number," I said quietly. I began sniffing continuously.

"Juan, are you okay? It's like one something in the morning. Aren't you coming to work tomorrow?"

"Ah, yeah, I'm coming to work but I need something to calm me down real quick. I need to get me a dime bag real quick," I lied. Not only was I lying about a dime bag but also I knew that it looked stranger because I didn't smoke.

"Juan, I know you're not getting this for yourself. You don't smoke," he growled in an angry tone.

"Please, Rob, I am twenty-seven years old. I'm not a baby and I don't need anyone telling me what I do and don't do. Just stay out of my business, please. Now are you gonna give me his number or not?" I was getting annoyed. He sucked his teeth as we sat in silence.

"Alright, girl, you got a pen?" he asked. I quickly grabbed my cell phone.

"Go 'head," I demanded. I rapidly keyed the telephone number into my phone.

"Got it, I'll talk to you later. Smooches," I said before the line went dead. I took another sip from the bottle followed by a hard swallow that burned the hell out of my throat. I felt the warmness in my chest and tried to gain composure without falling onto the bed. I dialed the number that Rob had given me.

"Yo," said someone on the other end of the phone. *Fuuccckk, I didn't even ask Rob his name.* I needed to think quickly and safely.

"Ayo, where da weed at?" I said, changing into my boy's voice.

"Who dis?" he asked. I closed my eyes hoping that I wasn't making a fool of myself. "Who dis?" he asked again.

"Yeah, dis J, from Southwest, where that weed at?" I was feeling the vibe from him. My buzz had already begun and I felt *good*. "My boy Rob put me on to you. Yo, I'm tryna be down."

"Aiight, shawty, I feel you. Check it. Come check me out in about twenty minutes down at Twenty-seventh and Snyder Avenue."

"Aiight, cool. You got me? You gon' look out?"

"Yeah, come check me out, kid."

"Aiight, I'll be there, aiight."

"Aiight, one."

I closed my cell phone and ran into the bathroom to dry my face. I looked at myself in the mirror for the last time before running into the bedroom to throw on some clothes.

Stephanie Mills filled the midnight air when I reached the George Platt Memorial Bridge. I sped through Broad Street cutting over to Snyder. Then I slowed down, watching the different hustlers stand on the corners through the darkness. The fiends were out shopping for their next hits as well. I approached a red light when I saw someone standing in front of a closed McDonald's. I pulled over to the side of the curb, wondering if it were wise for me to walk the streets asking for drugs.

I reached for my cell phone, then stepped out the car enabling the alarm.

"Yo, you got that hot shit?" I asked the dude that stood in front of the McDonald's.

"Naw," he stated, shrugging his shoulders. As the air became brisk I continued to walk the dark and lonely streets until I got

Twenty-seventh Street where I would meet Rob's connect for sure. About five guys were posted up on the corner standing on the wall of what seemed to be an old barbershop. I put on my George Jefferson stroll as I started to walk past them. A whiff of weed filled my nostrils as I strutted my stuff.

"You lookin' for something, homie?" asked a dark-skinned guy stepping away from the wall. As I stopped, my heart began racing.

"Yeah, dawg, I'm lookin' for dat *good* shit." I backed up to where he stood.

"Damn, I'm sayin' how much you tryna spend?" The other guys along the wall just looked.

"I got about two bills on me."

"Aiight, hold up a minute." He walked back over to the dudes who stood posted on the wall. All of them went into their pockets and gave the dark-skinned guy a few dice-shaped objects wrapped in saran wrap.

"Aiight, shawty, here you go but check it, my shit don't equal up to two bills but here's what I'ma do for you. I'ma throw in a couple shots of 'E,' aiight?" I went into my pocket to get my money before he placed everything into my palm.

"E?" I asked with a puzzled look on my face. He looked back at his homies, then at me.

"Yeah, 'E,' Ecstasy," he said, now talking with his hands. I still stood there with a look of doubt. I'd heard of the drug Ecstasy and had seen people take it but I'd never actually used it myself. Anthony used to take this shit all the time.

"Okay, cool," I said, taking the drugs and walking away. Anthony used Ecstasy but I guess it was now my turn to try something new.

After a visit to 7-Eleven for a few Dutches I made a stampede into my apartment. First and foremost I downed two E pills and replaced them with a mist of the *Angel* weed.

I lay in the bed watching an old episode of *Three's Company* where Terri was moving into the crib after she'd stuck that big-ass needle into Jack's ass. I always thought that she was the best looking out of the three blondes anyway. Those "E" pills had me feelin' it. My dick was rock-hard and this shit on TV was funny as hell. It was almost four in the morning and I was on my second blunt. I laced it tight, the way Bryant had laced it for me the other night. I got up and walked over to the mirror to admire my beautiful face and body.

For some strange reason my dick would not go down. I remembered the sexy-ass porn tapes I kept under my bed that sure were about to get put to use. I found the one that I liked. Tiger Tyson's fine ass was on the front. A nice Puerto Rican flick was what I needed. I popped the DVD into the player, sat down at the foot of the bed and released my monster from my boxer briefs. I hadn't given myself sex pleasure in a while and from the way these pills made me feel, this time would be very exciting.

I squirted some baby oil in the palms of my hands and thoroughly licked my lips. Tiger Tyson was banging the shit out of some dude's back. I began stroking my manhood back and forth and started to fondle my nipples. I reached over to grab the blunt and took another pull before my explosion. The faster Tiger pumped, the faster I jerked my dude. He was about to bust as I jerked faster and before Tiger had the chance to take off his condom, all the blood had rushed to the head of my penis and exploded onto my stomach.

My body fell back in the middle of the bed where I lay to

watch the rest of the video. Before I knew it the DVD was watching me.

$$$$$$

It was a quarter past twelve when I entered the salon. The music was pumping extremely loud and it seemed as if everyone including the customers had on loud colors. I said my "hellos" to the stylists and about twelve women sitting, waiting for their turn. I walked straight back into my office and closed the door. I sat down in my chair and threw my head down on the desk. I was alone for about five minutes before a knock came at the door.

"Who is it?" I growled, lifting my heavy head from the desk.

"Hmm, can I come in"? Rob said on the other side of the door.

"Come in," I responded, rolling my eyes up in my head.

"Girl, are you okay? You look like shit," he said, coming in and closing the door behind him. He came over and sat down in one of the red chairs at my desk.

"Gee, thanks," I spat sarcastically. "Can I help you with something?"

"Girl, I was just coming to see how you were doing."

"Don't you have a client in your chair?"

"Actually, I'm done with my client's hair. I also had to *wash* my client's hair too. What's happened to the so-called shampoo girl you hired? She hasn't been here in days." He was now giving me attitude.

"Look, Rob, for number one, I am the boss and you're the employee so calm your voice. For number two, thanks for checking up on me; and for number three, I don't keep tabs on Ieshia. I don't know where she is," I said, putting my arms in the air.

"Well, I'm sorry. Did you ever get in touch with Tony last night?"

"No, I never went to see Tony. I made me a cup of hot tea and went to bed," I lied, putting my head down and closing my eyes.

"Okay, well, I need to ask you for something," he said, getting up from his chair. I lifted my head to him and moved my hair from my face and tucked it behind my ears.

"What? What's wrong?"

"You made me the manager of Ché Mystic, so I feel like it is in this company's best interest if I make an educated decision," he stated, firmly standing in the back of the chair and pronouncing his words forcefully. I cuffed my hands on top of my desk.

"Okay, Rob, what is this 'educated decision' that *you* must make?"

"I think we need to let Jeff go."

"What do you mean we 'need to let Jeff go?' You're only saying that because you don't like him," I spat, coming to Jeff's defense.

"No, Juan, he's stealing,"

"Stealing what?"

"Supplies."

"Supplies, from me? How do *you* know?" I leaned back in my chair, waiting for his response.

"Well, you said yourself that once we take a job in your shop we cannot do hair on the side, am I correct?" I cuffed my hands over my belly, placing my elbows on the arms of the chair.

"Yes, you're correct." I nodded.

"Well, Kya and I have been witnessing him stealing *your* supplies at night, and he takes them home to use when doing hair at home."

I sat and thought about it for a minute before someone knocked on the door.

"Who is it?" I yelled to whoever stood on the other side.

"Juan, it's Jeff."

Rob's nostrils flared.

"Can I help you with something, Jeff?"

"Yes, you have a client out here waiting for you." I motioned for Rob to open the door. There stood Jeff with his hair coming down underneath a net hat. He was wearing a wife beater, capris, and a pair of dirty black-and-white Converses showing off his ashy ankles without socks. Once the door was opened he glanced at Rob and gave him a dirty sneer and then looked to me.

"Juan, you have a client that's out here waiting for you," he said, fingering behind him to the young girl. The girl made her appearance known by sporting a pair of black ruffled capri pants and a tight wife beater showing off her pregnant belly and a pair of State Property Keds. Her hair was pulled back Boned Snatch. And she wore a pair of dark shades.

"Yes," I spoke up, letting Jeff get back to his client. The girl walked forward looking a little old for her age. Her voice was very settled yet young-girlish.

"Yes, I had an appointment with you for today."

"Okay, I'll be out in a minute," I said as she turned and made her way back to the shop. Rob closed the door behind her.

"So, can I fire the bitch or what?" said Rob, letting the door slam. I got up from my seat and walked over to the mirror that hung next to the painting of Oprah Winfrey. I placed my hair in a ponytail.

"No, I'll do it. First, let me check into it and I'll let you know," I said, walking past him, opening the door and heading out onto the floor.

"You can come this way," I said to her as she got up and followed me to my chair.

"How do you want it?" I asked.

"Just a wash and curl."

"Oh okay," I said, walking to the shampoo sinks with her following behind. I turned around to prep the sink for her. I felt my eyes fill up with pepper spray, then a sharp foot landed directly into my balls when I fell to the floor.

"Bitch," yelled Rob when he ran over to me, pushing the girl out of the way. The entrance door swung open as two other girls ran in and started punching every client in the face who sat waiting to get their heads done. My eyes were burning heavy as Rob and the female began to get into an altercation. Words were exchanged. All I could hear were screams and girls yelling, "You fucking faggot."

Rob began waling on the little girl once I got up and maintained my balance. I started to swing with my burning eyes, not knowing who was getting hit. Girls were appearing from nowhere. More and more girls began to fight as I regained my eyesight. I ran in the back to get my baseball bat that I had stored in the corner just for something like this to pop off.

"Get the fuck out of here," I yelled, swinging the bat back and forth. The first time I swung the bat it landed on top of my workstation but the next time I swung, it landed right on the girl's back. Frustrated, Rob continued to throw blows at the girls as they came our way. Some of them backed up when they saw the bat I carried. The police were not too far so I knew that it was only a matter of time before they would appear.

By the time everything began to cool down, people were exiting my shop. Some exited with half of their hairstyles while others sat waiting, determined to get their heads done. I had flushed my eyes out with cold water as I was questioned by the police officers.

All the girls ran in different directions. The police weren't helpful to the situation at all. I decided from now on, instead of having a bat in the shop, I would carry a gun.

After stopping by the hospital to visit Anthony I went straight home. As I walked into the door of my apartment, my house phone rang. It was my mother.

"Hello," I greeted with caution.

"Hey, Juan, it's your mother."

"Hey, Mom, how are you doing? Is everything okay?"

"No, Juan, everything is not okay. If it was, I wouldn't be calling you." My heart skipped a beat a few times before it registered that she was being a bit shady. "Your father is sick. He's on his death bed and I would like you to come see him before it's the end," she added.

"Mom, what's wrong with him?"

"Well, for starters he has prostate cancer and the doctor says it's terminal. He has cirrhosis of the liver and his kidneys are failing terribly. Just get here as soon as you can," she said before hanging up the phone, leaving me dumbfounded.

I stood in the living room and thought for a minute about what had just happened. Out of all people, why would she call me and tell me about my father. I didn't care whether he lived or died. My phone rang again but this time it was Bryant.

I picked up the phone. "Bryant, where the hell are you?"

"Calm down, J.J., please calm down," he said, trying to state his case.

"No, I'm not gonna calm down. Where have you been the past two nights?" I got heated.

"J.J., would you calm down so I can tell you where the fuck I was."

"Where were you, huh?"

"I was locked the fuck up."

"Locked up, for what?"

"They're tryna get me for some dumb shit. Check this out, I wanna take you to dinner tonight," he added. I stood in the middle of the living room looking completely astonished. *Does he take me for some type of fool?*

"Bryant, where is my money?" I asked, cutting straight to the point. There was a bit of silence on the phone.

"Baby, I needed to use that money for bail. I'ma pay it back to you, aiight? I promise."

I sighed with relief. It wasn't that he had taken my money and run with it but I knew he had needed the money for a good reason.

"Okay, where are we meeting for dinner?"

"Meet me at Zanzibar Blue at seven o' clock sharp."

"You're talking about the one on Broad Street, right?"

"Yes, be there at seven sharp."

"Okay."

The sun was beginning to set when I left my apartment to meet Bryant downtown. I figured I'd wear something a little sexy, being as though he hadn't seen me in a few days. I sported a pair of khaki capris with the matching shirt and a pair of Steve Madden shoes.

I waited in the rush-hour traffic for about a half hour before reaching the restaurant. I had a valet parking attendant park my car while I went into the restaurant entrance. I walked inside to the atmosphere of live music being played by the Saint Nicolas Band and on every table there were cream-scented candles. The place was half-empty but at the bar there were people socially drinking; I presumed they were the after-work crowd.

Bryant sat far back into the corner wearing an army fatigue shirt with matching pants and cap. He sat grinning from ear to ear as I walked up to my seat and sat down.

"I'm glad you could make it," he said, lifting his wine glass to his lips. I began to smile as I sat down. There were two red envelopes with my name on them on the table.

"Are these for me?" I asked, picking up the envelopes.

"Yeah, J.J., it's all you."

"Hi, can I start you off with something to drink?" asked the white waitress who approached our table.

"Yes, please, I would like a Cosmopolitan," I stated.

"And would you like another glass of wine, sir?" she asked, looking at Bryant.

"No, I'm fine, thanks, just water." Once the waitress walked away I proceeded to look to see what was in the two envelopes. I pulled out the first card that said "Thank you" and the other card said "I love being your friend." I smiled at him when he reached across the table and planted a kiss on my lips.

"Bryant, what if someone sees us kissing," I said, blushing.

"I don't give a damn. Like I said before, Baby, *it's all you tonight.*"

"Well, Bryant, we need to talk," I said as the waitress came back with my drink and his water. She placed it down on the table and said that she'd be back to take our orders.

"Alright, I guess we do need to talk. Listen, I know I should've let you know sooner what was going on with me—"

"Yes," I interrupted. "You should've let me know everything that's going on with you. Shit, Bryant, I don't know shit about you," I added.

"What you mean you 'don't know shit' about me? You know enough." My face started to turn red. I tried my best to keep my voice down in the nice atmosphere.

"What the fuck do you mean I 'know enough'? I don't know shit about you. The only thing I know about you is your last name and I'm not too sure if I know the truth about that." He then reached into his back pocket and pulled out his wallet.

"Here, see. My driver's license." He reached across the table to show me his license. "See, I am Bryant Thompson," he added proudly.

"Okay, be that as it may. The only thing I know about you is your first and last name. I don't know nothin' else."

"Alright, J. Let's calm down. What do you wanna know?" I began to look around the restaurant seeing the after-work crowd expanding. I tried to focus on a couple of questions that needed to be answered.

"Well, for starters, where the fuck do you live and have you ever messed with a guy before?" He looked around the restaurant, hoping no one heard us.

"Can you calm down, please," he begged. "Now let's talk like adults."

"Okay," I agreed. "Where do you live?"

"Baby, I live in Southwest, Fifty-eight-twenty-four Chester Avenue," he said. "You don't believe me, do you?" He opened his wallet again to show me his address.

"Okay, granted. I know where you live but I don't know your past, your history, nothing." The waitress came back to take our orders as I did a quick overview of the menu.

"Are you guys ready?" She stood, holding her pen and pad. Bryant motioned for me to order first.

"I'll have the tender chicken roast with mashed potatoes," I requested. Bryant ordered the cheesy noodles. I was happy to know that it wouldn't take long so I could get back to scolding him.

"Now, you didn't answer my next question. Have you ever been with a guy before?"

"To finally answer your question, the answer is no. I have always been straight until I met you. I've always liked girls but for some reason your skin color and the texture of your hair made me attracted to you."

I smiled, then put my head down and blushed.

"Well, I try to take good care of my skin and hair just to get compliments like that. And furthermore I thank you for noticing."

"No need to thank me. All that is mine now," he said, waving his hand in front of my face. "I'm gonna make you a queen. Not just *a* queen but *my* queen. Do you have any problems with that?"

"No, no at all," I said, taking another sip of my drink while checking out his flawless skin and teeth; thinking of what would happen once we left this restaurant. The swell in the front of my pants told it all.

"Actually, I'm glad that you asked that question." He rubbed his chin.

"What question?" I asked with a confused look.

"The question you just asked. Have I ever been with a guy before? That was a good question."

"Why was that such a good question?" I asked with raised eyebrows.

"Because, I messed with a lot of females. Shit, I mean A LOT of bitches and none of them gave head like you." I almost choked on my drink from his comment. "I mean, you knew how to handle that ANACONDA. You really knew how to tame that thing. That's wassup," he said proudly as he sipped his glass of water.

"So, who do you live with?" I asked, jumping back to the subject.

"I live with my grandmother."

"Okay, where's your mother?"

"My mother passed away a few months ago."

"I'm sorry to hear that. Where's your father?"

"C'mon, J. You know a nigga never knew his father. I grew up in a single-parent household. My father was not around. Maybe I should be asking *you* the same questions. Where's your mother, father; shit, where's *your* family?" I gazed into his eyes over the calm flames of the candles and took a sip of my drink.

"My mother and father abandoned me when they found out I was gay. I don't have any brothers or sisters. How about you? Do you have any brothers or sisters?"

"Yes, I have a little sister. She's twenty-one. She's in college at Penn State. She lives in the dorm." He put his hands on top of the table as a signal for me to place my hands in his. I did.

"Hold up a minute." I hissed. "When I talked to you the other day you told me that you was with your shawty. Who were you with?" He began to laugh, covering his mouth with his hands.

"What are you laughing for? This shit ain't funny," I growled.

"Because you so cute." He stopped for few seconds and stared at me while biting down on his bottom lip. "It's so cute to see the jealousy come out of you." I sat there giving him the grizzly until he answered my question. "Man, you so funny. Sike, let me stop playing. When I said I was chillin' with my shawty, I was talking about my daughter, man."

"Daughter," I repeated with my chest getting warm from the drink.

"Yeah, my daughter." He stopped briefly to get serious.

"Bryant, I didn't know you had a daughter."

"Yeah, J., I have a seven-year-old daughter named Rain. I

hope she's not gonna be a problem." I was speechless. He saw the reaction in my eyes. "Is it gonna be a problem?"

"Why didn't you tell me you had a daughter?" I asked, giving him my full attention.

"Well, you never asked. Or I didn't think that it was anything more than sex with us. But now that I'm starting to get deep feelings for you, I would like you to meet her."

"What do you mean I 'never asked'? Don't you think that's something I should know beforehand?"

"Before what? Sex? I told you, I thought that sex was all we had, but now I'm catching feelings for you and I want you to meet my daughter. Is that okay with you?" I leaned back in my chair and scanned the room.

"Who's your baby's mother and are you still with her?"

"Her name is Melissa and no, I'm not with her," he stated as the waitress came toward us carrying our plates.

"This is hot, watch yourself." She set the plate in front of me, then set Bryant's plate down. "Is there anything else I can get you?" she asked, cupping her hands in front of her. We both shook our heads no as she smiled and walked away.

"Look, I was eighteen. I had just graduated from high school when Melissa got pregnant. We then broke up because she is crazy as hell. Rain was born and I always said that I would be there to take care of her. Now we're in a custody battle." He began to dig into his noodles.

"Okay. I'll meet her," I responded. He looked over at me with a sarcastic smirk. "What?"

"You want me to cut your chicken up for you?" He giggled.

"No, I'm a big boy, I can handle it." I placed the chicken in my mouth when his cell phone rang. He grabbed it from his pants pocket.

"This is my grandmother, I have to take this," he said, getting up and walking in the direction of the restrooms. I began to feel the vibe of the music that filled the air. Jazz was never my thing but I loved the way the band kicked it tonight. I found myself not thinking that much about Darnell while Bryant was in the picture and to be honest, the only thing I was really thinking about was getting home to taste some of my candy.

"J.J., come on, we have to go," raved Bryant who came back to the table tense and red-faced.

"What's wrong?" I demanded to know. He fumbled around in his pockets and threw eighty dollars on the table and grabbed my arm. Still I chewed the chicken and gravy as he dragged me from the restaurant.

"Baby, where did you park?" he asked with sweat beads forming on his head.

"I had valet parking. Bryant, what's wrong? What's wrong?" I gave the gentleman my parking stub.

"It's that crazy bitch. I'ma kill her," he growled. We both stood there anxiously waiting for my car.

"What crazy bitch?"

"Melissa."

"What happened?"

"I really don't know. All I know is my grandmother said that Rain was admitted into the hospital and she has to undergo surgery."

"Okay, Bryant, calm down." I turned to face him. "Where is your jeep?"

"I let my cousin use it. I took the bus here."

"Okay, take a few deep breaths." The valet drove up in front of us. The gentleman hopped out and Bryant and I hopped in. I jammed my foot on the gas pedal and sped off without thinking twice about leaving him a tip. I dodged in and out of the city traffic as I floored the gas pedal all the way down Broad Street. Rain was being seen at Einstein Hospital in the Olney section of Philadelphia. I had probable cause to run every red light that I came up against. Bryant's cell phone would not stop ringing and he had no intention to answer it. If it wasn't his grandmother, he wasn't answering.

I drove straight to the security booth in front of the hospital's emergency entrance.

"Baby, just go 'head in and I'll park the car," I said as he hopped out and closed the door behind him. I went to look for the first available parking space and pulled in on the side entrance. I parked and ran in, not knowing what had happened and whom I would encounter.

By the time I got to the waiting area Bryant had already gone into the emergency area. There was no staff in sight to answer any of my questions. In the waiting room sat an old, fat, black guy snoring loudly, and a white lady picking her nose sitting next to who I assumed was her son who looked very sick. I took a seat closer to the intake door, then began watching TV.

The doors opened and out came an elderly, heavy-set woman with her gray hair tied into a bun. She waddled with a cane as she walked over to the pay phone. I tried not to let her know that I was watching her. Clearly I saw the resemblance and knew that she had to be Bryant's grandmother.

"Shit, I need another ten cents," she whispered to herself, counting the change in her hand. She hurried over to the reception area where she found no one.

"Does anyone have change for a dollar?" she hollered over to the waiting area. The people that sat around us completely ignored her request. I stood up from my seat and reached down into my pocket and pulled out four quarters.

"Here you go, ma'am," I said, pouring the change into her hand and taking her dollar with the other. I could tell by the look on her face that she was completely stressed.

"Thanks, Baby."

I sat back down in my seat and began tapping my foot, wondering how long Bryant was gonna keep me waiting without a heads-up. I tried tuning out the sound from the television and the sounds of the old man snoring to hear her conversation.

"Hello, Matie," the gray-haired woman greeted in a weak, out-of-breath voice.

"That damn girl done lost her damn mind this time—I'm down here at the hospital with my grandson and great-grand. She's only seven years old and her mother is acting like a stone nut. She shouldn't be acting like this if she's planning to have another child. Last week the school called and said that she was suffering from dry eye syndrome. Bryant and I took her to see the eye doctor and they prescribed some eye drops for her." I pushed my chair over a little so I could eavesdrop better.

"So you know that Bryant is trying to gain custody of her. The other day when Rain came over, she had bruises on her arm from the beatings from her mother. I figured that that was only a mistake but this is the last straw. Now, this time that devil of a mother replaced her eye drops with Krazy Glue and now the poor girl's eyes are glued shut. The doctors are doing all that they can but most likely she'll be blinded for life."

I turned my body around to notice the lady sniffing and putting Kleenex to her nose. I wish that she knew who I was so I could've comforted her. But what I did know was that I needed to comfort Bryant later.

At a distance there was yelling and obscene language coming from the intake area of the ER. The doors busted open as a girl fell down on the floor with Bryant yelling and swinging his fist forcefully behind her. There were two police officers and a few nurses crowding the scene. The gray-haired lady immediately ended her call and hurried to see about the commotion.

"I'ma kill you, bitch!" Bryant screamed as he was taken away by the officers. The people in the waiting area got up to see what all the ruckus was about. The man wasn't snoring anymore.

"Bryant," I yelled with teary eyes. "Bryant."

"Let me go, I'ma kill that bitch," he yelled louder as the officers tried restraining him. The girl got up from the floor and stood in one spot, wiping off the bottom of her jeans. The closer I got to her I realized that she was the same girl who had come into my shop the other day.

$$$$$$

"Bail set at ten thousand dollars," said the redneck judge just before he banged his gavel on the desk. Bryant was being taken away by three county sheriffs for aggravated assault, simple assault, and resisting arrest. His grandmother almost fainted in the semi-crowded courtroom. I went over to her and gave her my hand to hold.

"Hello, Ms. Bernice. My name is Juan Jiles, I'm Bryant's friend." She took my hand as I helped her from her chair.

"Hey, Baby," she said teary-eyed. "I don't know what I'm gonna do now. His baby is very sick and he won't be able to do anything while he's in jail." I could see that this poor lady had been through a lot. From the sound of her voice she seemed weak and it was only a matter of time before she would break.

"Don't worry, ma'am, I'll take care of it," I said. She looked up directly into my eyes.

"How are you gonna take care of it, young man? I don't have that kind of money and I can't imagine asking *you* for the money. Besides, I don't even know you."

"Don't worry about it, Ms. Bernice. Bryant and I are real cool and I know he will pay me back the money when he gets it," I said in a sincere manner, hoping to calm her nerves.

"You're not a drug dealer, are you?"

"No, ma'am. I own my own hair salon down on South Street. I don't deal with drugs," I lied. Well, even though I didn't deal with drugs, I still used them. As we walked out the courthouse, a group of young girls was making their way up the steps.

"Hey, Ms. Bernice," said the petite girl with flawless skin and wearing a pair of Chanel shades. From her looks and her accent, I could tell that she must have been Puerto Rican. Her long hair landed on both sides of her shoulders as Ms. Bernice returned the greeting.

"Hey, Baby, how are you?" Ms. Bernice put her arms out to hug the pretty girl. "You're kind of late," she said, looking down at her watch. "They done set his bail already at ten thousand dollars," she added, embracing the pretty girl. The look on the girl's face was disappointment.

"Oh my God! Where am I gonna come up with that kind of money?" she asked.

"Oh, Baby, it's alright. This is his friend right here," she said, pointing to me. "His name is Juan and he's gonna front Bryant the money until he gets on his feet." The girl extended her arm to me as I put my hand out to shake hers.

"Hi, Juan, I'm Mariah—Bryant's fiancée," she said, shaking my hand as Ms. Bernice interrupted.

"Yeah, Juan, Bryant and Mariah are tying the knot next month. Did he tell you?"

VIII

DRAMA QUEEN

My heart fell to the pit of my stomach. I could not believe what I had heard. This bitch stuck her hand in my face showing off her perfect diamond. The smile on my face was a disguise against my broken heart.

"It's nice," I said, still smiling at the Rican girl.

"Isn't it nice," Ms. Bernice agreed. "What time are you gonna go bail him out, Baby?"

"I'm gonna go to the bank now and then down to the fifteenth district and pay the bail. "

"Okay, Baby. I'm gonna go on over to the hospital and check up on the baby. I'll see you there."

"Ms. Bernice, do you want me to come along?" asked Mariah, tailing behind.

"No, no, Baby. You go on home and get some rest. I don't need another one of my great-grands in the hospital," she teased. I began to chuckle a bit. *What does she mean by another great-grand?*

We all parted our ways as I made my dash into my car. I sat behind the steering wheel thinking how I could be so naïve. When I was seventeen Father Tyrell would always tell me the heartaches and the bullshit that I would have to put up with when dealing with a so-called straight boy. My eyes began to water as I thought about the nice dinner we'd had last night.

We came clean about everything and now that bastard was engaged. How so?

I neatly wiped my eyes clean before pulling out of the parking lot. Being as though things weren't going my way anyway I felt as though I could take my time bailing his ass out. Now that I knew who the girl was that came into my shop the other day, I could officially bring charges to her ass. I went down to the twenty-second district station and filed charges on her for assault and terrorist threats. Then I went past the salon to make sure business was running as usual.

By the time I got to the bank it was half past three. It was extremely crowded; I wrote my name down on the sign-in sheet and took a seat until my name was called. After about thirty minutes a light-skinned gentleman called my name.

"Mr. Juan Jiles," said the gentleman. I got up from my chair and began to walk toward him. He extended his hand to shake. "Hi, I'm Rasheed Winters, how are you today?" he asked, leading the way to his desk with me following behind.

"I'm fine actually. It's a nice day outside." He went to sit behind his oak desk as I sat on the opposite side. A tall, slim, young, corporate-type guy was what I needed in my life right now because these thug niggas were not cutting it.

"So what brings you in today?" I loved the way his eyes connected with mine. If only he knew that with every word he spoke, I would take those words and transfer them into my own fantasy. *How would you like to kiss my lips? Let's get away to a weekend in paradise.* I immediately snapped out my trance and focused on what he really was saying.

"Oh, what brings me in today?" I repeated trying not to sound stupid. "I need to make a large withdrawal."

"Oh, you're going on vacation," he said, turning toward his computer to look my number up in the system. I handed him the piece of paper with my account number written on it.

"No, not really. I wish I was, I need the money to get my brother out of jail," I lied.

"Oh okay, I don't mean to be in your business. I'm just trying to make a little small talk, that's all."

"Oh no, I don't mind," I said, staring into his dreamy eyes. I could tell that he had my account up on the screen by the size of his eyes once he saw the figures.

"Okay, Mr. Jiles. How much are you planning to withdraw today?"

"I need about ten thousand five hundred, please."

"Okay," he said, going into his top desk drawer and pulling out a form. "I need you to fill out the top section and I need two forms of I.D. and you're good to go," he added.

I filled out the paper and gave him all the necessary credentials he needed to process my transaction.

"Thanks, I'll be right back." He got up from his seat, letting his long pole become visible through his tan slacks. He walked around his desk and over to the teller area to retrieve my funds. Sitting in this atmosphere brought memories into my mind. I could remember it all as if it was yesterday. My man, the gun, the shooting, the yelling. This wasn't something that I was proud of. It was something that happened due to my man's greed. Sitting there I allowed myself to rethink every aspect of that day from us leaving the house together to me leaving the bank alone.

"Here you are," said Rasheed, walking behind his desk taking a seat. He handed me a lightweight envelope. I grabbed it and opened it to find a cashier's check in the amount of $10,500.

My head started to spin as I snatched the envelope from the desk and stormed out, thinking about what I'd just found out about Bryant and Mariah and how pretty she is. I rushed to my car, started the ignition and pulled out of the lot. I drove to the corner and pulled over to the curb. I was contemplating doing something that I never had done before. I didn't have any weed and along with that I didn't have a Dutch either. I reached down to the sides of the car door where I kept my stash of candy.

I looked to see about four rocks remained in the clear plastic bag. I began to crush each rock down to a powdery substance and placed a line on the back of my hand. I looked around to see other cars speed by as I inhaled the entire line of candy. My head spun rapidly out of control as I felt my body being pushed back into the seat. I sat there for about an hour getting myself together. And before I knew it the sun was setting and the moon made its appearance in the sky.

As I sat still in my car, I felt like I was moving at a full speed like eighty to ninety miles per hour. I saw my whole life flash before my eyes. I was high but not just off the white stuff I had snorted; I was high off life.

This drug had taken me back to a place where I didn't want to be. I sat there in the driver's seat, looking straight out the front window as if I was watching a movie. I saw my dad come into my room at night after my mother would go to sleep.

$$$$$

"Did you get your allowance for this week?" he'd ask as I sat up in my bed wiping the cold from my eyes.

"No, Daddy, I didn't. But I did everything I was supposed to do. I

swept the kitchen floor and mopped it and I took out the trash." He *started to walk closer toward me and by that time my eyes were fully opened.*

"Dad, can I ask you something?" He was standing in front of me in his boxers.

"Sure, peanut head, what do you want?"

"James and Larry are having a sleepover and I was gonna ask Mom but I knew she'd say no, so I'm asking you. Can I go?" I asked in a childlike manner.

"Well, I don't know, can you?" he asked as I sat there in my bed with a confused look.

"What do you mean, can I? I'm asking you, can I?"

"I'll put it like this." He walked toward me and sat down on the bed next to me. "The answer lies in you; whether or not you should go. All you have to do is your deed and I'll let you do whatever it is you want." He leaned back as his pole started to stand at attention. He looked at me and nodded his head in the direction of his penis. I knew from that point on if I did what he wanted me to do then he'd let me do what I wanted.

"Juan, do you remember sucking on your mother's breast when you were young?" he'd ask.

"No," I answered.

"Well, you wouldn't remember because you were young but back then that's how she used to feed you with milk."

"Oh yeah, I know because Aunt Ada does that sometimes with her baby. She breastfeeds her baby through her chest to create milk," I said excitedly because I knew what he was talking about.

"So now act like my penis is your mother's breast, or better yet, act like it's a baby's bottle and you're a baby and suck it until milk comes out of it." He removed his dick from his boxers and held it in both

hands. I thought about it for a second and that particular night I hadn't had dinner so I thought if I sucked my dad's penis it would fill me up. It didn't. Instead it brought me a lifetime of heartaches and broken promises.

Still feeling weary, I managed to drive myself home without any luck of Bryant coming home today. I went home and went fast to sleep.

$$$$$$

The phone rang loudly awakening me from my good night's rest. I continued to lie in the bed and let the phone ring. I jumped up and reached over to grab the cordless from its base.

"Hello," I answered in a raspy voice.

"Yes, is Mr. Juan Jiles available?" asked the voice on the other end of the phone.

"Speaking."

"Hello, Mr. Jiles, I'm so sorry to wake you. This is Doctor Watson from Pennsylvania Memorial Hospital. Anthony Wright has you down as his next of kin." I jumped out of the bed, trying to gain my visual sense to see what time it was. The clock read 3:41 a.m. "It is very important that you come to the hospital's ICU immediately."

"Why? Is there something wrong?" I asked in panic mode.

"Yes, we are having a slight problem and need to operate. In order for the operation to take place you will need to come sign the papers."

"Okay, I'm on my way," I said, walking through my dark room stumbling over clothes and shoes that lay on the floor. I threw on a pair of sweats, some sneakers and a baseball cap, jumped in my car and sped off.

The main entrance was closed so I had to walk all the way around to the emergency room entrance. I checked in at the front desk, letting the nurse tell me the direction of the intensive care unit. I took the elevator to the fourth floor where I met Anthony's doctor.

"I'm so glad that you could make it on such short notice, Mr. Jiles," said the elderly white-haired doctor sporting a long white coat.

"That's okay. What's wrong?"

"Follow me, Mr. Jiles," he said, leading me down the hall into a small room with a wooden table and two chairs. I sat down at the table as he closed the door and joined me at the table. He laid a folder on the table containing a few sheets of paper with Anthony's name on them. He lowered his head and took a deep breath.

"I'm gonna give it to you straight. Both of Anthony's kidneys are failing so we're gonna have to do an emergency transplant. If the surgery is not done within the next forty-eight hours he could die." I placed my hand over my heart as my eyes began to water. I was speechless.

"How? I mean what?" I said, trying to get my words in order. "What do I need to do?" He placed his hand over mine.

"You will need to sign a few forms giving us permission to operate. But Mr. Jiles, that is the least of your concerns." He looked directly into my eyes. "Can you or do you know anyone who can donate a kidney to him? We would have to run tests to make sure that there is a match though. Maybe we can get lucky right away."

"No, he doesn't have any family. I'm the only one," I stated with tears running down my face.

"Well, Mr. Jiles, I'll tell you what I can do for you. I will make a few calls to some of my colleagues with the hopes of putting Anthony's name at the top of the transplant recipient list." My heart became heavier than it was before.

"I really would appreciate that," I said as he gave me a tissue to wipe my nose.

"But for now we need to keep our fingers crossed, okay?" I shook my head in agreement.

"Is Anthony awake? I mean, can I see him?"

"Not at this time. ICU does not allow visitors at this hour but you are welcome to see him first thing in the morning."

"Thank you," I said, getting up prepared to leave.

"Mr. Jiles, I need you to sign these forms before you go."

"Oh, I'm sorry." I grabbed the pen and signed my name on the highlighted lines.

$$$$$

I was able to pay Bryant's bond with the actual check that was given to me by the bank. The clerk at the front desk said that he would be released at noon. To pass the time I figured I would go by the salon to make a few quick extra bucks until Bryant called me to let me know he was home.

"Damn, look who decided to make her appearance at Ché Mystic today," joked Rob as I walked in the door carrying a box of donuts. "Oh, and she brought snacks," he added.

"Shut up," I hissed. "Today is not the day," I said, piercing him through my shades.

"Um, excuse me." He proceeded working on a girl's micro-braids.

"Hey, Juan, how are you, sweetie?" Ieshia asked, shampooing an elderly woman's hair.

"I'm fine, girl, how you been?" I walked straight to the back, carrying the two dozen donuts.

The shop was packed with wall-to-wall customers. Hopefully doing a few heads and laughing and joking with my staff would help take my mind off Anthony. I placed the boxes of donuts on the table next to the coffee maker.

"If anyone wants donuts, you can help yourself," I said, licking the excess sugar from my fingers. "Oh, that's my jam. Can you turn that up, Jeff?" The loud sounds of Ciara's "Goodies" filled my ears. I began to dance when a few customers decided to join in.

"Alright, girl, I see you," yelled Rob from his corner. "Do the booty dance." Kya came to the center of the floor and took her turn imitating Beyonce by doing the booty dance. We all laughed.

"No, I'll show y'all bitches how it's done," teased Rob now taking center floor. He turned around and started making his ass cheeks clap.

"Aww shit," yelled the girl that sat in Jeff's chair. Rob continued to do the booty dance in the middle of the floor, waving his arm back and forth holding a handful of weave. I heard my cell phone ring from my man bag. I ran to grab it, hoping that it was Bryant.

"Hello," I answered, walking into my office and closing the door behind me.

"Hello, Mr. Jiles. This is Doctor Watson. Did I catch you at a bad time?"

"No, how are things going with Anthony?"

"Well, I have good news. We found a donor. I'll start Anthony's operation immediately."

My eyes lit up with glee. "That's great."

"So, I will give you a call first thing in the morning."

"Okay, thanks for calling." I ended the call. I could still hear the music pumping from the other side of the door. *Thank you, Jesus.* I said a silent prayer as someone knocked on the door. I opened it.

"Guess who," said Rob, standing in front of a young woman. "Someone's here to see you," joked Rob. It was the one and only Mary as in Mary J. Blige. She stood next to a man who looked to weigh 300 pounds.

"Are you the owner of this salon?" she asked. She looked stunning in a pair of blue jeans, black knee boots and a pink tee as she eyeballed me over the top of her sunglasses.

"Yes, I am. How can I help you?"

"I'm only in Philly for one night and I can't find anyone to do my flips the way I need them to be. Can you help me out?" She looked at me through her golden-brown shades.

"Sure, Mary. Take that seat right there and I'll hook you right up." I pointed to my station.

Once Mary was in my chair I decided to open the floor up for a little conversation.

"So what brings you out to Philly today?" I looked around to see if I had her color weave in stock.

"Eve is having one of her famous fashion shows at the Convention Center tomorrow and I came down to show her support, ya know," she said as she made herself comfortable in my chair.

"You know, I'm looking forward to that next album, girl."

"Yeah, me too." She giggled.

"What's the title of this album?" I asked, hoping that she would let the cat out of the bag. You know some artists don't want the public to know anything about their next project until it actually drops.

"Well, actually, I'm still working on my Love & Life tour and that album just dropped so I won't be working on another one for a while."

"Oh yeah! *Love and Life*. Ayo, Mary, that shit is hot." I gave her dap. "First of all, I love the cover where you show a little bit of your stomach and love the tracks three, nine and seventeen. Yo, track number seventeen. 'Special Part of Me' be having me in my room crying sometimes. Like I really be needing someone to hold me," I explained.

"Yeah, it's a good feeling when you finally find true love. It gives you a warm feeling inside." She took a deep breath and smiled as she was definitely in love. At that point I really needed to change the subject because I was starting to think about Darnell and now Bryant. And that shit wasn't cutting the mustard.

Throughout the day and as time began to wind down I still hadn't heard from Bryant. I stayed behind to catch up on some overdue bills after sending my stylists home. I sat in my office writing out checks to the electric and phone companies. I balanced my checkbook and made sure that Uncle Sam got his cut. I began to take inventory to account for the missing items that Rob had witnessed Jeff taking.

It seemed a bit ridiculous after ordering twenty bottles of shampoo to have had stock run out in a little over three days. Even a few of the hairbrushes were missing. I noticed a few combs missing as well. I wrote each missing item down on a sticky note and attached it to my computer monitor to remember to address the situation on our next business day. I was contemplating calling Ms. Bernice because I knew that if Bryant were released he would have called me by now.

I stared at the phone on my desk hoping that it would ring. I even checked my cell phone to see was it on and it was. The clock slowly approached ten p.m. with my mind going in a frenzy to be kept waiting. I quickly searched my phone book for Ms. Bernice's number.

"Hello," she answered in a sleepy voice. I paused for a second before saying hello because I knew that it was kind of late to be calling someone's grandmother.

"Hey, Ms. Bernice. It's Juan, Bryant's friend."

"Yes, Baby."

"Yes, I paid Bryant's bail earlier today and I was wondering how he made out. He didn't call me. I was thinking maybe his paperwork got mixed up or something. Has he called you?"

She didn't hesitate to answer my question. "Yes, Baby. Bryant has been home since around three o'clock. He came in and got in the shower and left. He's probably out with his fiancé somewhere. I think they might have gone baby shopping. You know he spoils that pretty girl of his."

My heart pounded in my chest. I couldn't get a word out. I could feel the blood rushing through my body and settling into my face. "Since three o' clock?" I repeated to make sure I was hearing correctly.

"Yeah, it was about three because *General Hospital* was on. I'll have him call you when he gets in."

"Okay, Ms. Bernice," I stated firmly before ending the call.

Furiously I quickly cleaned off my desk by throwing everything that wasn't useful to me in the trash. I grabbed my cell phone and dialed his number rapidly. He was sure to get a piece of my mind at this very moment. My chest burned like hell, waiting for him to answer. I held the phone close to my ear as I began to walk through the salon turning out all the lights. By the time I got to the entrance door his voice mail was answering for him. I chose not to leave a message because I wouldn't dare give him the satisfaction of hearing the sound of my voice in this heated state. As I closed my phone the ringer sound startled me as I checked the lock on the gate for the last time.

"Hello," I said grizzly, holding the phone up to my ear.

"Damn, Baby, it's nice to hear your voice too," Bryant said playfully from the other end. My heart felt relieved from the stress but at the same time hot from his tone.

"And where the fuck have you been?" I shouted, looking down at my watch, holding on to my man bag and getting my car keys out all at the same time.

"Damn, what, you keeping a lock on me now? I'm out chillin' with my boys, J. Look, don't start trippin'."

I disabled the alarm on my car and stepped in. "Out with your boys, where?" I was getting heated about why he hadn't checked in with me first, as I had paid his bail.

"We goin' down to Delilah's, a gentlemen's club, for a while and then I'll be by to see you, aiight?" His voice was getting low. I smiled. "You goin' wait up for me?" he added.

I started the ignition to let some time pass before giving him an answer. "You know I will," I responded in the nick of time before he began talking.

"Aight, I'ma holla at you aiight. One." The phone went silent. I sat in my car, letting Gerald Levert take me back with the words of "Casanova" as I made my way through the nightlife of Philadelphia. The thought popped into my mind about taking in a visit to see Anthony. But, at the same time, I hadn't been out for a night on the town in awhile so I called up a few of my old friends to see what was poppin'.

After scooping up Sketchy, one of my old classmates, we decided that we would make a night of it and pay thirty dollars to attend the Prodigy Ball being held at L&J Hall in the heart of North Philly. I loved having Sketchy with me, especially at times like this because he made me laugh.

"Bitch, it is on tonight," he yelled from the car as I sped through the streets. For this occasion Sketchy wore a pair of extra-tight jeans to show off his stacked physique. He also sported a pair of navy blue-and-black Steve Maddens, a skintight shirt that was covered by a brown leather ski jacket that complemented his light-skin tone. On a night like tonight and with the way I was feeling I needed to be around someone like him. This was a person who is very loud and who liked to make me laugh; and that's one thing that Sketchy was—LOUD.

By the time we reached the ball, the House of Prodigy was taking center floor walking their runway as a house category. The theme for tonight was "Wine and Crystals." Every member from the house either wore the color of red wine or a heavenly color of white crystal. And all of the pretty boys strutted their stuff, taking the runway wearing wine-colored thongs. I felt the throb of my chocolate stick through my jeans. But to keep things simple, my stick would only beat for one man.

"Work, bitch," yelled Sketchy as he snapped his fingers as the mother of the house made her way down the runway. The DJ played the old Cheryl Lynn classic, "Got to be Real." The crowd was hyped and the ball had officially begun. After about forty-five minutes of standing in the cut the commentator called out the face category for the House of Labuchi and of course, I took center stage.

I walked the runway with both of my hands on my hips while smiling from left to right. The crowd of spectators clapped as if they appreciated having my face grace them with its presence. I smiled enjoyably on the outside but my heart was beating miserably on the inside. I began licking my teeth back and forth and by the time I got to the end of the runway before the judges, above all the screams and the chants, I could hear Sketchy in the background screaming, *"That's my muthafuckin' sista."*

I stood perched on the side of the judges as I waited to see who was gonna step forward trying to give me a run for my money. I counted silently in my head as the suited-up commentator held his microphone close and called out the competitors' names.

"Oh, y'all faggots are scared of Miss Juan tonight," yelled the commentator. I glanced to the side to see my entire house members chanting our slogan: "L...A...B...muthafuckin' ...U...C...H...I" as they snapped their fingers. I blinked only a few times to see who was gonna take stage. Then immediately my heart fell to the pit of my stomach when Bryant came out walking toward me from the back of the room.

"Aww shit, Juan, I think you betta move over." The commentator looked at me, then back at the fine hunk of a man that took the runway. The closer Bryant came toward me the sexier he looked. At about a quarter of the way he stood and ripped his T-shirt off his back as the crowd gasped at his shining six-pack.

"Oh, daddy, put the head in," screamed the commentator as the pit of my underarms began to sweat. I could feel my blood pressure storming through the roof as I saw my nigga flossing in front of these faggots. I couldn't take no more. I ran over to him and grabbed him by the arm.

"C'mon, shawty, what you doing?" he spat. "Let me go."

"What the fuck you mean, let you go. NO," I said enraged as I pulled him from the runway. "You told me that you were going out with your boys."

"I am out with my boys," he yelled, pointing in the direction of the House of Karan.

"What?" I yelled.

"If y'all gonna argue, take that shit outside. Y'all shouldn't bring your problems to the ball. Settle that shit at home," stated the commentator as the music stopped. Sketchy ran over to me.

"Bitch, you didn't tell me that your man was a piece of trade, a down-low brotha." At that point I was furious.

"C'mon, Sketchy, let's go," I yelled as I finally let go of my grip on Bryant. As I prepared myself to walk toward the door I felt a shooting pain in the back of my head. I turned around to Bryant giving me three left hooks.

I tried my best to fight back but then the next thing I knew the whole House of Karan started in on me. I was receiving blows from every angle. People were pulling my hair and kicking me in my stomach. Sketchy ran to my aid, trying to help me off the floor.

All I felt were the stings from my bottom lip. Unbeknownst to me Rob was there. He ran over to me, wetting a paper towel with a bottle of water, and gave it to me for my lip.

The crowd began to scatter as I gained my composure and limped toward the door. I left L&J Hall with my face throbbing and knuckles bleeding. Rob and Sketchy walked with me to the car as the commentator continued. "DJ, pump the beat."

IX
A Thug's Passion

"Hello."

"Hello, Mr. Jiles."

"Yes, who's speaking?"

"Hello, Mr. Jiles, this is Rasheed Winters from SunTrust Bank. How are you?"

"I'm doing well, thanks for asking. How can I help you?" I said trying to focus my eyes on the clock to check the time.

"Well, I was calling to follow up on you to see how things are going. Because when you left out of here the other day you were pretty upset."

"Things are going fine, thanks."

"I kinda find that hard to believe," he stated.

"Um, excuse me?"

"No, I'm saying, you sound a little troubled."

"Um, Mr. Winters, you said your name was."

"Yes."

"Do you always call to check up on your customers?"

"Only if I take a certain interest in them I will...I took an interest in you. Well, let me be forward with you. When you came in the other day I must say that I noticed you noticing me."

"Excuse me? First of all, what gives you the right to be going into my personal file and getting my phone number to call me? And second, if I was troubled, which I am *not*, that's none of your business. Good-bye."

"Excuse me, Mr. Jiles, first of all, I was being nice and second, you're as *FAB* as you *think* you are. And *third*, as of next week, if you don't have a payment into us we *will* foreclose on your shop. Now *you* have a good day, Mr. Jiles." *Click*. The phone went dead.

Some nerve of that bank freak to call my damn house questioning me. And what the fuck does he mean they will foreclose on my shop. I wish they would.

I got up from the bed and walked into the kitchen and poured myself a nice glass of Merlot. I sat down on the couch trying to recollect what had happened the previous night. The wine helped take away some of the pain in my face but what I really needed to numb me was a few pieces of candy. As I sat and drank my troubles away I let my tears fall.

I looked around my living room and asked myself what had happened? What happened to the love that I once shared? What was left of my life after Darnell's death seemed to shatter once I opened my salon. This is not how things were supposed to end. That afternoon I sobbed. I sobbed like there was no tomorrow. What was eating me up on the inside was finally making an appearance on the outside. I got up and walked over to the stereo and played one of my favorite CDs, *Somewhere in my Lifetime* by Phyllis Hyman.

I sat there on the living room floor with my back against the wall and continued to let my tears flow. The words that Phyllis spoke cut so deep down into my soul. I closed my eyes and en-visioned myself playing with my mother when I was younger; the love that my family once shared with me before this lifestyle came into play.

"I miss you, Mommy and Daddy," I said aloud as Phyllis took

me away with her words about living all alone. The tears fell from my eyes like a raging waterfall. "Darnell," I screamed to the top of my lungs. The tears fell more.

"Oh, my God. What happened?" I asked over and over again. "My life, what happened?" I held my head down as the music continued to play while I sat and sipped the last of my drink.

By the time Phyllis was telling me that the answer was me, the phone started to ring.

"Hello."

"Hey, Juan, it's Trudy from downstairs. You have a guest here to see you. Ieshia?"

"Yes, you can send her up," I responded cheerfully, wiping the tears from my face. I quickly hung up the phone and tried to straighten up the mess I had made. I was very excited to be sharing human contact. I really missed being around her, plus we had a lot of catching up to do.

The doorbell rang and I anxiously opened the door to see her standing, holding a bouquet of approximately two to three dozen roses. She was standing in a flowerbed of multicolored roses with a trail of more roses behind her leading to the elevator where Bryant stood.

Almost immediately my eyes began tearing all over again. Ieshia stood smiling without saying a word. I looked her up and down, then down the hall to Bryant where he stood also holding a bouquet of roses with a blank look upon his face.

"Good afternoon, sunshine," Ieshia said before Bryant began to take his first step. I backed up in the doorway, feeling tipsy from the glass of wine I had downed. "Can we come in?" she asked. I backed away to make room for her entrance as Bryant hurried toward the door.

"Baby, I'm sorry," yelled Bryant as Ieshia entered my apartment. By the time Ieshia stepped all the way in Bryant was standing directly in front of my face. I looked him dead in his eyes, noticing the scratch below his right eye from where I'd scratched him the night before. I began to close the door slowly as he stopped it with his foot. I glanced down at his feet, noticing him sporting a pair of fresh shell tops without any socks.

"What, Bryant? What do you want from me?" Ieshia stood behind me in total silence. "After what you did to me last night, you think I'm supposed to forgive you?" He stood there speechless. "And not just about last night. Nigga, you was released from prison and you didn't have the respect to call me and let me know you were home. You're a sorry-ass nigga," I hissed. If no one had ever heard a pin falling onto the carpet, then now was the time.

"Juan," Ieshia said firmly. I turned around to stare in her direction.

"What, Ieshia? You don't have anything to do with this."

"I know I don't have anything to do with this but you listen to me and listen to me clear." She stared me straight in the face without blinking. "You have a man that made a mistake and is man enough to admit his mistake and say he's sorry for what he did to you."

"Now I know that just because he was fuckin' high off some shit I don't even care to know about, does not give a reason for what he did. And he's standing in front of you feeling every regret for *doing* what he did doesn't make it right." She set the flowers on the loveseat.

"But what I'm *gonna* say is that you have a man standing in front of you. I don't have one. I wish I did. But *you* do—and my suggestion to you is if you love him the way you say that you do, then you will put up with the good times as well as the bad times. Shit, I been with Antwoine four fuckin' years and he never did no shit like this for me. Even after I put up with all his shit and, on top of that, the nigga is gay," she said in a raised tone. I tried my hardest to keep my laugh in but I couldn't. I even heard Bryant chuckle a bit.

I stood there motionless, hoping that neither one of them saw that I was actually breaking down and considering the things that Ieshia had said.

"And you know I'm right; that's why you're still standing there," she added. I took a deep breath and turned back around toward Bryant. I moved out of the way to let him in and I shut the door behind him.

"Now I'm gonna leave so y'all can make up or do whatever it is that y'all do. Juan, I'll be at the shop if you need me." She walked up to me and planted a kiss on my cheek before walking out of my apartment. I turned toward the door without taking my eyes away.

"So do you forgive me?" Bryant asked, standing in a hooded sweatshirt, capris and shell tops. My emotions ran crazy as I turned around and walked slowly into his arms. He dropped the flowers on the floor and embraced me like I had dreamed. I squeezed him tight and held on for dear life, not wanting to let go. Ieshia was right; I had a man right here.

"I'm sorry, J.J.," he said. I let him go long enough for our lips to lock as we began to tongue wrestle. I grabbed the back of his head and tried to force him into my mouth with all my might. We backed up enough for him to lay me down on the couch. He climbed on top of me and started grinding as he began kissing all over my neck and chest. He forcefully sucked my neck, leaving a deep-red hickey, then proceeded to mark the other side.

"I miss you so much, Baby," he moaned erotically as he pulled up my shirt and commenced to licking all over my chest, my stomach, then planted his tongue deep into my belly button. I let out a few moans when he helped me take off my shirt. He then lifted me up and carried me into the bedroom where he wanted to do the honors of undressing me himself. He pulled every item of clothing from me with his hands until he got to my boxer briefs. With them he wanted to take them off using only his teeth.

After he pulled my underwear off with his pearly whites, then tossed them to the floor, he stood up to remove his hoody, sneakers, and capris. His pole stood rock at attention pointing forward through the slit of his boxers. I stretched out on top of my queen-size bed waiting for what I had been craving for over a week. My body needed this right at that very moment. I thought about the way those faggots had chanted over my nigga's body last night at that ball. Those faggots only dreamt about having a man like mine. Once he was fully undressed he leaped onto the bed to finish what we had started in the other room. I sucked on his lips like a Hoover vacuum, tasting everything that he'd had for breakfast.

He then stood up as I knelt down so I could lick all over his *Thug.* I let the firm mushroom head hit the back of my throat as I deep-throated him lovely. I sucked, sucked, and sucked some more, making love to his dick with my tasty tongue letting all my saliva drip down his shaft, causing him to arch his back like a cunt.

I grabbed his butt and jammed his love stick down my throat as hard as I could, letting him know that after all that had happened I was in control.

"Damn, Baby, that's wassup. Eat this dick, kid," he said provocatively. His ass muscles flexed with every gag. "Let me get on top," he said as he got up to get in the position to begin tea bagging me. I laid my head down on the pillow and watched him as he positioned himself over my face. I was in paradise as he dipped down, letting his hairy balls lay on the tip of my tongue. Before I realized it, his entire sac had filled my mouth.

"Sit up and let me fuck ya face," he said as we switched positions for the third time. I leaned up with my back against the headboard as he pulled my head closer to his torso. He filled my mouth up with dick, dick, and more dick. I closed my eyes as he made love to my mouth as if it was teenage girls' pussy. The headboard banged heavy against the wall as I could hear the old lady beneath me banging on her ceiling with a broomstick.

"Man, fuck this, I'm ready for some ass," he said as he forcefully pulled me down onto the bed as I held my legs in the air and he began to penetrate me with his tongue. First he started from the bottom, then worked his way up my crack. I moaned with ecstasy and pleasure from his ever-so-warm tongue. I licked my lips back and forth while he thoroughly sucked my rectum. I had never been turned out like this before. Darnell had never come close to what *this* nigga was doing. I mean Bryant's tongue was going up, down and around inside my love tunnel. He even stayed down there forty-five minutes longer than Darnell ever did. I closed my eyes and licked my lips and imagined my thug tasting me for dinner. He almost made me cum just from him eatin' my ass. Now that's some fly shit.

He continued to munch me for about another fifteen minutes in between stopping and letting me know that I tasted *sooooo good*.

"Damn, Baby. You got me," he said, taking his right hand and slapping it against his chest. I smiled at him as he lay on top of me while inching his way inside of me.

"*Ahh*," I moaned when I felt him enter me. He started slow, then proceeded to move faster. As he stroked more, his speed increased. I moaned every time his sausage went in and out my dookie cave. I grabbed his back and held tight as the headboard banged back and forth from the wall. The lady downstairs drilled the broomstick in her ceiling with every stroke.

"*Ahhh*," was the only sound that I could manage to escape my mouth. "Bryant, I think I'm about to come," I screamed as he stroked harder.

"Bust that nut, nigga," he said softly as his breath brushed past my ear. The silence of my apartment was broken due to the headboard hitting the wall. And the old lady beneath me wasn't letting up with that broomstick either. As we both fell on our sides Bryant grabbed my dick and began jerking me off while banging my back out. And I must say that it would be an understatement if I said that the feeling was *GOOD*.

"C'mon, Baby, let's bust together," he yelled. I could not resist myself from letting my angel cream ooze all over my clean linen.

$$$$$$$

It had begun to rain and after my baby came shortly after I did, we lay there in the bed as he lit a Dutch while we talked.

"Damn, shawty, that shit was on point," he said as he exhaled the smoke from his mouth and nose. He lay back on the bed as

I laid my head on top of his chest playing with his tiny chest hairs.

"Bryant, can I ask you something?" I said still playing with the curls on his chest.

"What's up, J.? It's your world, boo."

"What do you really think about me?" He took another long drag on the blunt as I waited patiently for an answer.

"Hmm, what makes you ask that? You know how I feel about you."

"I know but after last night, I have doubts now and even so, I wanna hear you say it."

He leaned down and kissed my forehead.

"On the real, shawty. I think I'm falling in love with you." I couldn't see the expression on his face when he said the words I was waiting to hear. But my heart melted as he spoke his words carefully.

"J.J., do you know that you're the only dude that I ever messed around with?" he said as I got up from his chest to rest my head on my elbow so I could look him in the eyes. Just looking into those big browns made my dick hard all over again.

"Well, actually we never talked about that. But since you brought it up, I didn't know that. Which brings me to another question," I said as he placed the Dutch in between my fingers so that I could take a pull.

"And?"

"When did you join the House of Karan?" I inhaled the blunt and held it in my mouth for a second before releasing the smoke in his face.

"Well, to answer your question, I'm not in the House of Karan."

"Okay, so why did they attack me the way they did?" I said, giving him the blunt back from my sore lips.

"Because I got paid to walk that ball last night and when you approached me, that fucked shit up for me and the person who paid me. You have to think, a lot of them faggots like me. They would kill to be in your place right now. They wanna suck this big dick." He grabbed his big pole and held it straight in the air.

"So you're telling me that you really didn't know them like that?" I was giving him my undivided attention and looking at the veins in his penis at the same time. My mouth watered just looking at it sitting pretty on top of his pubic hairs.

"Fuck no, I was tryna make some extra ends. Look, J, I'm not into this whole gay shit like that. Check it. I'm a muthafuckin' nigga who likes bitches but happened to fall in love with another nigga. That's how I look at it," he said, now trying to get the rest of his high out of a roach.

"So what were you high off last night?" I asked out of curiosity but I soon realized that it was curiosity that killed the cat. He turned and sat the roach in the ashtray on the nightstand by my bed. He then turned back to me.

"Look, J, the shit that happened last night I regret doing. Baby, can we put that shit behind us? Please?" I stared into his big browns.

"Okay, Bryant, I understand. But you still didn't answer my question," I hissed.

"Look, J, if I tell you, will you put this shit behind us and move on?" I took a deep breath hoping I could stomach the shit he was about to confess to. "I was on some PCP shit."

"What? Bryant, how much of that shit did you take?" I snapped. "And you were Xanied up too?"

"Baby, calm down. Look, you don't understand," he stated loud and firm, getting up from the bed. He sat on the side of the bed with his head in his hands. I moved the covers from on top of me and sat directly behind him rubbing his back.

"Bryant, something's not right. Tell me what's wrong. Boo. I'm here for you." He held his head down, looking at the floor when he started sniffling as if he were trying to hold back a few tears.

"J, that bitch killed my baby," he blurted.

I didn't understand. Once again my heart failed at what he was trying to explain to me. "What bitch? What baby?"

"Melissa, she was pregnant with our second child. And she went and had an abortion." He looked up at me with tears in his eyes. "J, it was a boy. It would have been my first son. Little Bryant," he explained.

"Hold up. I'm not following you. How do you know if it was a boy or a girl? I mean, how many months was she?"

"Baby, she was seven-and-a-half months' pregnant."

"I didn't know that people could still have abortions that late in their pregnancy," I said.

"Really you can't, but if you do decide to go that route, then it's more money. She paid close to nine hundred dollars to have that abortion to spite me." He got up and walked over to retrieve his capris that lay on the floor. He picked up his pants and pulled out some Polaroid pictures.

"See, this is what that slimy bitch did to my son," he said, throwing the pictures on the bed. I picked up the three pictures and carefully looked at them to see a small baby's head turned completely around from his body. The other two pictures showed the baby's neck broken in three different places.

"Bryant, what the fuck is this? Where did you get this shit?"

Totally naked, he walked back over and sat in front of me on the bed. "She sent these pictures to my grandmother's house after the procedure was done."

"I didn't know a person could do that. How could she?"

"She did it to get back at me because one of her friends came in your shop and overheard your stylist talking about me. That's how she found out who you were and where you worked." I threw the pictures down on the bed in disgust. *How could a person be so cruel?* I thought.

"Now, that's why I been so fucking stressed and doing crazy shit." He took the pictures from the bed and threw them on the floor.

"Baby, I'm so sorry that you're going through all this," I kissed the back of his neck and rested my head on his shoulder. "Wait, while we're on the subject of baby's mothers, who is Mariah and is she pregnant with your child?"

He let out a slight giggle, then looked toward the ceiling. "Look, J.J., Mariah is my girl, okay?" He now turned to face me. "Let me explain this to you." He grabbed both of my hands and placed them in his. "I am a straight dude. I'm a straight dude that fell in love with another dude. Now I can't have the reputation of a fag or some bullshit-ass sissy dude. I can't let my family find out that I'm dealing with a dude and not only that, but as much as I love you, boo, I still like bitches.

"The bottom line is, I still want to be with you. But I am building a life with Mariah and, yes, she is having my seed."

I looked up to the ceiling trying to hold back my emotions. I couldn't help but let the tears fall. The thought of sharing my man with someone else was dreadful.

"J, I'm not trying to hurt you. That's the last thing I wanna do. But I need you to feel me and see my point." I brought my eyes down to face his. "Do you feel me, boo?"

I couldn't believe that I actually understood where he was coming from.

"Yeah, Bryant, I understand. But why didn't you tell me?" I said, now letting the tears fall.

"Because honestly, Baby, I wasn't gonna tell you. I wanted you all to myself without having to think that you thought about me being with someone else. But, baby, I will promise you that my straight life will never interfere with my life with you," he said, tickling my torso, making me giggle. I leaned over and planted a kiss on his pink lips. We talked for a little while before it was time to begin round two.

$$\$\$\$\$\$\$$$

"Hey, sweetie," I said to Anthony as I gave him a lovable kiss on his cheek. "You're looking well," I added.

"Thanks, why did you leave me here for a whole week alone?" he asked in a groggy tone.

"I'm sorry, Anthony. But I knew after the surgery that you needed your rest so I made sure that you got it. How did everything go anyway?"

He formed his hands as to say *whatever*.

"It was so-so. I have a long scar in the middle of my chest. Wanna see?" he asked, smiling at the gesture.

"No, I think I'll pass," I kidded.

"Oh, since *you* weren't here, I did have a visitor," he said as his pretty face lit up.

"Oh really, who?"

"Reggie."

"Reggie?" I asked, trying to recollect my thought as to whom he was referring to.

"Yeah, Reggie. The guy I introduced you to at your party."

"Oh, how is he?"

"He's fine; he came a few days ago and kept me company. He calls a lot too."

"How did he know that you were in the hospital?" I asked, getting up to get a brush from my bag.

"Chile, these are faggots. You know word gets around."

"Well, it seemed like you haven't done shit with your hair. Let me at least brush it for you while I tell you what's been going on with *me* lately," I said as I began brushing his hair.

"Girl, spill the tea. I have been out of the loop kinda long so please catch me up. Especially on that sexy-ass man of yours. When am I gonna meet him, anyway?"

"I don't know but I'm sure it will be soon. How long did they say that you have to stay in here?"

"Well, my doctor wants to keep me here so he can run a few tests on me. I've been feeling a little weak lately so he wants to keep me here for observation."

I continued to brush Anthony's hair. The grain seemed softer than normal like it was thinning and getting ready to fall out.

"Damn, girl, when was the last time you combed this shit?" I teased.

"I don't know. I have a good mind to cut all this shit off. I'm getting tired of all this anyway."

"Well, you better do something. I'm sure Reggie doesn't like seeing you this way."

"Juan, at this point, it doesn't really matter."

$$$$$

After spending my morning with Anthony, I made my way to work just in time to have a nice talk with Jeff. When I did my count the other day I noticed that more items were missing. I needed to make a decision and make one fast.

I sat at my desk going over the inventory count again. I didn't want to fire someone for no reason and I didn't want to make it seem that I didn't believe Rob either.

"Rob, after you finish your client's shampoo, can I see you in my office a minute," I said, trying to over talk the sounds of the radio.

"Sure, give me about five minutes," he responded with both hands full of shampoo. The good thing about getting rid of one employee was that I could afford to make room for Ieshia. I sat behind my desk and thought about the plans that Bryant and I had made for the evening. Tyler Perry was bringing his play *Madea Goes to Jail* back to Philly and I had gotten us tickets. After that I had planned to take him to a nice dinner at the SoHo restaurant on Broad and Walnut. Then we could take a romantic stroll along Penn's Landing.

"The queen is here," hollered Rob from the other side of the door.

"Come in," I yelled. He opened the door, walked over to the chair in front of my desk and sat down with his legs crossed.

"Well, aren't you just a pretty one today," I teased as he wore a pair of denim capris for the first time.

"Yes, chile, you like?" He sported a big smile.

"I must say that I do and I'm also feeling this new curly look that you got going on," I said, pointing to his head. He grabbed one of his curls and pulled.

"Yeah, I'm going for a new look. What's up?" He gave me his full attention.

"Well, the reason I called you in here is because I would like to shed light on a situation you brought to my attention last week and take action," I stated firmly giving him direct eye contact. "And since you're the manager of Ché Mystic, I would like you to be present as well as testify."

"Well, you know a girl don't have shit to hide and a bitch ain't scared. Bring it on," he said as he snapped his finger in my direction. I got up from my seat and walked over to the door. I opened it to find Jeff sitting in his chair listening to headphones and reading the paper. I pointed at him to get his attention and asked him to come into my office.

"Shut the door behind you, please," I said, taking a seat behind my desk. "You can have a seat," I offered, pointing to the chair next to Rob who continued to sit with his legs crossed as he rested his folded hands on his knee.

"No, I think I'll stand for this one," he responded.

"Well, certainly. Jeff, it has been brought to my attention that as well as working in my shop you also have your own thing going on once you leave here. Is that true"? I asked, cutting straight to the point.

He paused for a minute and looked down at Rob, then at me. "Yeah, that's true," he said, smacking his lips.

"Okay, Jeff, are you aware that my policy states that if you are a stylist in my shop, then you cannot moonlight?"

"Yeah, I know the policy but I needed some extra money so I did what I had to do."

"Okay, also it was brought to my attention that you're taking supplies from this shop home so that you can moonlight. Is *that* true?" My eyes were dead set on his as he switched them from me to Rob.

"You know what, Juan? Some people in here need to mind their fuckin' business," he yelled as he swung his fist into the back of Rob's head.

"What the fuck…," yelled Rob when Jeff hopped on him and he fell forward into my desk, causing it to push back as Jeff continued to wale on Rob's head and back with his foot.

"Get the fuck out my office," I screamed as Rob tried to gain balance to get up from the floor. When he finally did, he began to reciprocate on Jeff as they both knuckled up in my office causing the desk to turn over with my monitor from my computer falling on the floor. Rob threw Jeff against my water cooler causing my painting to pop from the wall.

Keisha and Kya ran into my office as I yelled for someone to call the police. Rob had Jeff penned against the floor as he continued to wale on him.

"Get the fuck off me, bitch," yelled Jeff in between taking Rob's licks. Each time the word *bitch* came from Rob's mouth the more times his fist met Jeff's face. I ran over to grab Rob's arm to lighten up the blows to Jeff but I wasn't helping. Rob began to squeeze Jeff's neck as an encore before he would let go.

He then pushed Jeff's head with a mighty force a final time before letting go and leaving the room. Jeff continued to lie on the floor in a comatose state.

"Rob, you have to leave because when the cops get here they're gonna lock you up," I said.

"No, fuck that…that bitch swung on me first. I was just defending myself," he said, placing his hands on his hips and trying to catch his breath.

Within minutes the police were entering my shop for the third time and Ché Mystic had only been open for a month and a half.

"Sir, what seems to be the problem?" asked a Caucasian cop, chewing gum and coming toward me with his right hand on the handle of a pistol that was tucked by his waist.

"Two of my employees were fighting," I said breathing heavily. The phone rang.

"Keisha, could you get that please?" I yelled.

"Who started the fight?" asked another officer as he walked around the perimeters of my overturned desk. This officer was black. "Get an ambulance here," he said on his walkie-talkie.

"Well, I was about to terminate the employee that is lying on the floor. After I questioned him about some missing items in my shop, he then got violent," I said.

"So what you're telling me is...the guy that's lying on the floor started the fight?" asked the black officer. I then looked up at Rob to make sure that we made eye contact. *You got my back and I will have your back.*

"Yes," I said as I watched Rob who still seemed to be breathing heavily.

"I can't breathe," said Jeff to the white officer as he gasped for air. The paramedics rushed their way into my shop that I called a salon. Keisha's and Kya's clients sat in their chairs astonished. The people who stood out front looking in were disappointed when I closed the door to block their view.

"Juan, Bryant wants you on the phone," yelled Keisha. I ran over to Rob's station and picked up the cordless.

"Hey," I answered cheerfully.

"J, what the fuck is going on there?"

"The manager and one of my employees got into a fight, that's all," I explained.

"You aiight?"

"Yeah, I'm fine but my office is a mess. What time are you comin' through?" I asked, trying to drown out the sound of the paramedics as they began to carry Jeff out.

"I'll be there around eight, I'll call you later," he said, hanging up the phone before I could respond. I pushed the "end" button on the phone as the white officer came over to me to make a statement.

Once everything was done I walked back into my office to a mess of disarray. Papers that were very important to me were lost in a pile of ruckus. My desk was overturned with water spilled through the grains of my cherrywood panels. I couldn't deal with what was set in front of me at that second.

"I'm going out to lunch. Look after the shop," I said to Rob as I grabbed my man bag and walked out of the salon as if nothing had happened. My stomach was empty because I was hungry; not for a meal from McDonald's but for what the person who stood in front of McDonald's had in their stash.

I stopped by the ATM on Broad and South and withdrew four hundred big ones. When I got back to the shop, I was gonna be full from what Rob's connect had in store for me on this day—guaranteed.

X
HEARTBURN

"Yo dawg, check it. How much you got?" asked a tall light-skinned gentleman that Tony had made connections with. He stood about six-one of pure solid muscle. I could tell that he must've recently gotten out of jail because he had that look—clean cut with black, shiny waves flowing through his head like an ocean.

His hairline flowed into sideburns that connected so gracefully to his beard, which lined up so well with his mustache. He stood posted up on the side of the McDonald's wall wearing a pair of tan khakis rolled up at the bottom with a pair of black Air Force Ones sporting an oh-so-fresh wife beater. He handled my money very delicately when I placed the entire four hundred in the palm of his hand.

"Here's four hundred dollars but I'll bring you back a little more later. What can you give me for this?" I asked, turning around to the streets to see if anyone I knew spotted me. I couldn't believe that I was doing this in broad daylight but after what had just happened I needed a lift.

"I got you, hol' up," he said, taking my money and stuffing it into his pocket. I waited on the side of the building while he walked around in the parking lot to his car. After about fifteen minutes he returned with a small brown paper bag full of all kinds of goodies and treats for me.

"Ayo, what's ya name, dawg?" he asked me while looking dead into my eyes.

"Just call me J.J."

I took the bag and walked quickly toward my car. I hopped in and sped off down Broad Street. I rode all the way until I got in the back of the Wachovia Center where all the concerts are held. I remember one time when I was in high school I took some dude in the back of the building and sucked him off real nice. He was the star of our high school basketball team and almost every time I saw him in school he would wink at me.

Well, even though he was dating one of the baddest honeys in school, she wasn't giving him what I could give him and he knew it. He made it his business to meet me in back of the Wachovia Center every Thursday after seven in the evening. I could feel the precum rising to the forefront of my dick just thinking about it.

I pulled all the way around to the back where other than someone emptying a bag of garbage, no one would see me. I pulled over to the side of the car where the sun had gleamed down on the top of my head, causing my activator to shine more. I opened my bag of goodies and smiled as I sniffed the contents containing so many biohazardous materials to get me well on my way. I took out the first lump of white grain wrapped in Saran Wrap and opened it to watch the substance take a breather of the fresh air.

I got my hands on a crispy twenty-dollar bill and twirled it ever so tight until it was as tight as I could get it. I always watched movies where people had done this and once in a while I'd see Bryant do it before our sexcapade. I lined the sweet candy on the front of my makeup mirror and, without any hesitation I sniffed the entire line of the bill as each substance glowed through my nose straight to my membrane.

"Aww" was the sound I made as the candy shot up my nose to my brain. My head bounced back onto the headrest with a little snot still hanging from my nose. I wiped my nose on my sleeve with the back of my hand. I sat in my Lexus coupe with my head down. The wind blew through my window as my car stood still. I was in my zone. I overheard the birds chirping along with the whistle of the trees. I felt the burning sensation in my brain.

Just that fast, all the uncontrollable bullshit that had gone on today was controllable. Everything was okay. The man who shot me out of his dick was now dying of cancer but that was okay. Everything was okay. The mess that I left in my office wasn't so bad that it couldn't be handled. I felt very sleepy. All I wanted to do was rest. I grabbed my cell phone from my man bag and called the salon. Rob picked up on the first ring.

"Ché Mystic, how can I help you?" he greeted.

"Hey, Rob, it's me, Juan," I responded in a slurred tone.

"Where are you? That muthafucka is talking shit. Talkin' 'bout he gonna bring his cousin up here to kick my ass. Where are you?" he yelled.

"I was calling to tell you to close the shop tonight. I won't be able to make it," I said, hoping that I could get off the phone without him having further questions.

"I will but I'm telling you now, that piece of shit better not come back here with no dumb shit or she's gonna get knocked." Before he could go any further I closed my phone. I then opened it to give Bryant a call.

"Yeah, what's up," he answered.

"Hey, Bryant, it's me."

"Me? Who the fuck is me?"

"It's me, Juan. What, you don't know my voice?"

"Fuck no, nigga, you sound fucked up. Where are you?" he asked as if he were laughing.

"I'm about to go home. I was letting you know that I'll be there instead of the salon."

"Aight, I'ma come through like eight or nine. What you got for me tonight? What's so special that you must see me tonight?" He sounded like someone was trying to get his attention in the background.

"I wanna go see a play with you tonight; that's all. Who is trying to get your attention?" I asked, getting a sense of where he was.

"Naw, that's my bull. I'll be at your crib lata. Aiight?"

"Bryant, I…"

"One," he said before hanging up the phone.

I put the key in the ignition and fired up my Lex with the hopes of going home to get prepared for my evening with Bryant.

By the time I got home it was already a quarter after five. I took the stairs to my apartment because the elevator was on the outs. By the time I reached the top, the effects of my candy were wearing away. So after opening the door of my apartment, I stormed in the kitchen to catch another buzz. But this time I decided to take two of the little green pills that were also in the bag and, instead of snorting my candy, I smoked it.

I sat on the couch in my boxer briefs feeling lovely. I put the table fan on rotate so that it could rotate my high all around the room. I sat the Dutch in the ashtray and lay back on the couch.

Bang, bang, bang. "Open up, it's the police," yelled the officer.

I jumped up from my couch in complete darkness and immediately looked over at the clock that read 12:55 a.m.

Bang, bang, bang. "If someone's in there *open the door,* if not we will force our way in." I ran over to the door in my boxer briefs and opened the door.

"Okay, now step away from the door," said the officer who I could not see due to the bright flashlight in my face. "Have a seat on the couch," he said, walking in slowly with about ten officers following behind being escorted by two dogs.

"Is there a light in here?" asked one of the officers.

"Yeah, right here," I said, turning on the switch from the lamp that sat on the end table next to the couch. "What's the matter, officer?"

"Is this your apartment?" he asked with the flashlight still shining in my face.

"Yes."

"Are you a drug dealer, sir?" asked the officer who looked as if he could be a redneck.

"No, sir."

"Do you run drugs for someone?" He looked down at the brown paper bag that sat on the coffee table that I'd brought in earlier.

"No, sir, I don't deal with drugs," I lied. He walked over to the bag as my heart thumped with every step that he took. He picked up the bag and sniffed it before looking in it to see the contents.

"You lied to me. That's not good," he said before turning around to face the other officers. "Let the dogs loose," he demanded as two of the other officers did as they were told. I sat on the couch shaking as the dogs ran loose throughout my apartment with the cops following them.

"So do you use drugs, sir?" the redneck-looking officer asked me as he handed the brown bag to an officer who seemed to be of higher rank. The other officers flooded my apartment with their bodies.

"Can I go put something on?" I asked the officer.

"No, you stay right there. Is there anyone else in the apartment with you?"

"No, I'm here alone," I responded, hoping that this was some type of misunderstanding.

"Does anyone else live here with you, sir?"

"No, I stay here alone."

"We found something," yelled an officer from my bedroom. "We found something in the closet." The dogs began to bark loudly as I sat on the couch, shaking from the hallway draft.

"You wait right here with him," said the redneck to another officer before he and the captain walked toward my bedroom area. I sat on the couch, dazed and confused about what they could have found in my bedroom.

Three officers walked from my bedroom and into the kitchen and threw about four shopping bags on top of my glass table.

Boom! I heard the bags as they hit the table. I tried my best to stretch my neck to look but I could not see anything. The redneck came from the kitchen and back into the living room where he was removing his handcuffs from his pouch.

"Please stand up and put your hands behind your back." He grabbed my arm to help me stand.

"Am I being arrested, officer? What am I being arrested for?" I said as chills started to creep down my spine. Never in my life had there been a time when I was placed in handcuffs. The dogs and the other officer came walking from my bedroom and now were going in and out of the hall closets.

"You're being arrested for possession of cocaine and marijuana, drug trafficking with the intent to distribute," said the redneck, tightening the metal cuffs.

"What? Sir, I don't know what you're talking about. I don't have any drugs here."

"Yeah, well, a few kilos of cocaine and marijuana bags on your table tell us otherwise." He pushed me toward the door as the other officer and the residents who lived on my floor watched. I was being taken out in my underwear without any clothes. I had never in my life been so humiliated and embarrassed.

"May I ask where you're taking me?" I said with the redneck rushing me down the hall.

"You're going to jail."

"*Jail!*" I yelled. "For how long? I have a business to run."

"Well, tonight you're going down to the police station and you have to have charges officially brought up on you. Then you will be booked and you will go in front of a judge first thing in the morning and he will set bail." He literally dragged me onto the elevator, out of the door, and threw me into the car. Tonight of all nights had a cool chill in the air and me not having on any clothes didn't help me get comfortable.

I recollected my thoughts. Bryant and I were supposed to go out tonight so that meant he never called. *How did the drugs get into my house and who the hell put them there? It must have been Bryant and he must have done it while I was sleep.*

"Can I make a phone call?" I said to the redneck once we got to the station. I was about to have my picture taken and be finger-printed.

"In a little while," he said. My feet were as cold as ice as I sat on the cold bench admiring my heels ash up. I was in desperate need for some lotion. I sat in the cell and laid my head back onto the cold wall. The cell was no bigger than my bathroom. I would say maybe eight-by-ten feet. I didn't know what was in store for me at this point. Maybe I was set up. Maybe the drugs were always there even before I had moved into the place.

"Mr. Jiles," the officer said.

"Yes."

"We're ready to start the booking process now," he said, taking one of his big metal keys and unlocking the cell door.

"Can I ask you a question, officer?"

"Sure."

"I know that you said that drugs were found in my apartment but where specifically where they?" I asked.

"They were in the floorboards in your closet. You should know, you put them there," he said sarcastically.

"No, I did not put them there."

"Well, look, don't say it to me, tell it to the judge." He closed the cell door and grabbed my arm and walked me toward a camera. I held up a blackboard in front of me that stated my name and birthdate along with a few other numbers beneath my chin. He took about five pictures, one from each angle, then led me to a table to be fingerprinted.

"Can I make my phone call now?" I said after the fingerprinting process was over. He led me into a little room that had a wood chair and wood table with a phone on it. I sat in the chair.

"You have five minutes," stated the redneck before closing the door. My first call was to Bryant's cell phone.

"Yerp," he answered in a sly tone.

"Hello, Bryant. It's me, Juan," I said quickly before the phone went dead. Astonished by what had just happened, I hurriedly dialed his number again.

"Yerp," he repeated.

"Bryant, don't hang up. It's me, Juan." The phone quickly went dead again. After trying for the third time the phone went straight to his voice mail. I didn't leave a message; instead I called Rob.

"Hello," he answered.

"Hey, Rob, it's Juan."

"Bitch, where the hell are you? It's coming up unknown on my caller ID and you know I don't normally answer unknown numbers, girl."

"Listen, Rob, I'm in a lot of trouble and I need your help," I stated as quickly as I could before my call time was up. "I'm in jail and instead of opening the shop tomorrow, I need you to come down to the court at nine thirty at City Hall."

"Girl, what have you gotten yourself into?" Rob hissed.

"I can't explain right now. So we're gonna close the shop for tomorrow and I also need you to call all of our appointments for tomorrow and reschedule."

"Well, bitch, for one thing you're about to pick your mouth up off the floor because tomorrow is the Alicia Keys concert and she has an appointment scheduled for four-thirty. And today, after you left, two guys came in looking for you and I told them that you weren't in so they gave me an envelope with a paper in it addressed to you. Do you want me to open it?"

"No, not right now. Just call Alicia Keys' contact person and tell them you apologize for the inconvenience and tell her that we owe her one. Shit, if you have to, send her next door to Chez Sonia's."

"Time up," said the redneck as he stood outside the room watching me through the window.

"Okay, Rob, I gotta go. Make sure you're down at City Hall tomorrow by nine thirty sharp."

"Okay, I'll be there," he confirmed before the line went dead.

The redneck escorted me back to my cell where I would spend the next six hours shivering in my boxer briefs.

He closed the door behind me as I took a seat on the concrete bench where I was supposed to lie down and get a good night's rest. *I think not.* I said a prayer to God asking Him to get me out of the situation. I had to be set free because there was nothing for me to be guilty about. I had done nothing wrong. I hadn't stashed any drugs in the floorboards of my home. I decided I would lie back and think of all the good times in my life. The first thought that would always pop into my mind was when I was a child and the way my mother always would hold me in her arms and rock me back and forth with the notion that everything would be okay.

See, in my household we grew up like the kids on TV. I guess you could say that we were the Huxtables. My mother would stay home and cook and clean and take care of the house until my dad came home from work. Well, we weren't so much the Huxtables; more like the Cleavers because my dad was not a doctor and my mother was damn sure not a lawyer. And of course we didn't have all that damn money.

I'm not saying that we grew up poor either but we always had. Whenever I needed something, whether it was for school or something I wanted to have, my mother and my father would always try to make a way for me to have it. Even though it got lonely sometimes, I loved being the only child because there wasn't enough love to go around. There was only enough love for me. Those were the good old days before my dad starting flipping out when he'd come home from work to catch me playing Double Dutch with the girls instead playing ball with the guys.

One time, when I had to be about seven or eight years old, I was sitting on the steps playing with my cousins minding my own business. On that particular day I was more excited than any other day because my cousin Simone's mother had brought her the new Malibu Barbie for her birthday and she said I could play with it. I would style the doll's hair in styles that hadn't even been invented yet and I made sure that doll had on the flyest clothes to match. I had created my own fantasy in a Barbie. My Dad strolled up the street coming from work, sipping his can a beer through a straw as usual. Sipping a can of beer through a straw was my dad's MO.

"Jay, I know you're not doing what I think you're doing," he yelled as he walked quickly to where I sat. He threw the can of beer into the street as he continued to walk in my direction. I tossed the Barbie behind me in total fear before my dad came up to me, gripped me by my neck and squeezed as hard as he could before letting me go. My body dropped back down onto the steps.

"Boy, what did I tell you about being out here playing with these girls? You're supposed to be playing with boys. Ain't no son of mine gonna be a sissy, do you hear me?" he yelled as he forcefully slipped off his thick leather belt without missing a loop.

The first whelp hurt the most as he caught me right across my chest. My eyes immediately filled up with tears as I began to holler out for my mommy. Simone dropped her doll and backed away as I got my ass whipped right there on the steps. My mother flew from the house holding a dishtowel in her hands.

"Earl, what are you doing to that boy?" she yelled.

"I caught him playing with dolls. You were here, you should've stopped him," he yelled up to her as he continued to wale on me.

"Stop hitting him like that," my mother demanded as she stood at the top of the steps.

"Mom, Mom," I screamed louder and louder hoping that she would come save me from this humiliating episode.

"Brenda, shut up before I come up there and start beating on you," he yelled. After he had gotten tired of beating me, he picked me up by my stinging arms and rushed me up the steps. He then threw me in the house on the floor and began beating me some more.

My mother walked back into the kitchen and finished doing the dishes.

After that tragic experience between my parents and me, there was no more late-night rocking in the chair with my mother. There were no more bikes and nice toys that parents give their children at Christmas. There was nothing but lonely silence in the Jiles house from my age of eight until I turned fourteen.

By the time I turned fourteen and was in middle school, I was too young to work, so I went to my father to talk about the issue of allowance. At that point I began to think that I was the reason for my family's dysfunction and that the only way I could make it right and gain allowance was to go back to my roots. Being as though he was my father there was nothing I could do but to respect him, fear him, and do what I needed to do to keep him happy.

Along with me taking health class in school he also explained to me the process of conceiving and delivering and where exactly babies come from. He explained that a baby comes from a womb that lies inside the mother but he also explained how the seed is injected inside the mother. The seed is injected into the mother through a man's penis, which in this case, that man was him. So he said I was disrespecting the root of a man by doing girlish things. Going back and making things right with the root would not only make it better but I could start receiving allowances.

The root ended up being his penis and I needed to kiss, caress, and suck it every night before bed. My duty also was to never let my mom find out about what was happening.

Four years later, after telling my psychology teacher what was going on, she then got in contact with my mother. My mother didn't want to hear any more of the lies I had been telling my teachers at school. So she immediately packed my things and set them out on the doorstep by the time I got home from school. Since then Tyrell Karan had been the one father I knew and cared about. He'd made sure I always went to school and kept clothing on my back, even if he'd have to craft them.

I remember walking my first ball. Tyrell said he wasn't gonna let me walk until I was ready; he'd never force me to walk, I would do it on my own. Back then I was flamboyant but not as flamboyant as I was now. Tyrell taught me to be myself under any circumstances and that's what I did. The flashy lights and the colors and the big crowds at the balls didn't intimidate me. I was taught to go in there and do what I had to do to win and get my trophy. It was never a jealousy thing for me because I knew I had the cutest face and I was always confident that I would win.

All around me were nothing but a bunch of faggots; I'm talking old queens, young queens, or just queens who came out to fuck or get fucked. It didn't matter to me. I started from the beginning of the runway and sashayed to the judges' panel where the famous Aiyana Kahn, John Karan, Meechie Laquai, Dwayne Milan, Mann Prodigy, Joey Revlon, and Sania Ebony sat waiting to judge my face for the first time ever. I watched her close as Aiyana waved her fan back and forth in front of her face sporting a pair of oversized Gucci glasses and a long weave giving off the Cher look.

Aiyana was the mother of the House of Kahn, which is a house that started in D.C. with her and Father Charles. Aiyana was born a male but had female organs and she was FIERCE. Her beauty could match a straight woman's any day. Mother Aiyana was known in the ballroom scene for her beautiful face and Father Charles was known for his fierce voguing. The rest of the Kahn members were known as their angels. At the end of the runway, they all sat side-by-side waiting to see how much face I had; whether or not I had any scars, moles, and being as though I was young, I didn't have to worry about them judging me on razor bumps.

I glanced across the panel as each judge took a hard look at my face, neck, and teeth. But before I knew it I had competition standing next to me—some dude from the House of Prodigy named Jason. Jason was a little shorter than me and we both had the same caramel complexion except most of mine was natural and he was painted. Jason had a lot more spunk than I did but due to my flawless looks the commentator told us both to stand to the side while the panel judged us individually.

I stood waiting while the crowd went wild over Jason's face.

I watched his house members chant their house name, "P-R-O-D-I-G-Y." But by me being a new face, I had no one tooting for me but my good ol' Father Tyrell. After the judges were finished with Jason it was now my turn. Father Tyrell had taken me under his wing so I now had the entire House of Karan chanting my name. Within a matter of minutes throughout all the noise and the cameras and the people, the judges chose me and awarded a trophy that stood almost the same height as me. I was flattered to know that my face was good for something other than putting lotion on in the morning. Then from that day forward everybody in the ballroom scene knew my name.

$$\$\$\$\$\$$

It was half past nine when the sergeant called me in for court. I was led into a small courtroom with my hands and ankles shackled as if I were some type of murderer. Rob sat in the back of the room wearing a skin-tight T-shirt and a pair of light-tinted shades with a confused look upon his face. I nodded to him, thanking him for making his appearance. At the time he seemed like all the family I had.

I walked up to the bench where a white gray-haired man sat back in his chair with his arms folded. After the clerk sat the necessary paper work down on his desk he then lifted up and placed his glasses on his face as the sergeant came and stood by my side. By that time Rob had already gotten up to search for a closer seat in the courtroom.

"State your full name, sir," said the gray-haired judge.

"Juan Jamal Jiles," I responded, looking him dead in his eyes with my hands cuffed to the front.

"Do you know why you're in court today?" the judge asked now sitting with his hands folded on top of the desk.

"Your Honor, I'm really not sure but I do have an idea, yes," I responded.

"Mr. Jiles, this is an arraignment held today for the charges that were filed against you in the state of Pennsylvania. Do you understand?"

"Yes," I said, standing there still in a pair of boxer briefs and a pair of slip-on socks that were given to me at the police station.

"Okay, you have the right to remain silent. Anything you say or do will be held against you in the court of law, Mr. Jiles. Do you understand that?"

"Yes."

"Okay, Mr. Jiles. If you choose to give up that right, everything you say *can* and *will* go on record. You have the right to an attorney; if you choose to give up that right, one will be appointed to you. Do you understand? May I proceed?"

"Yes."

"Mr. Jiles, you're being charged today with the following… Three counts of drug possession, which is a felony and can carry a minimum of jail time of five years and a maximum of thirty. Three counts of drug trafficking, which can carry a prison term of two years to ten years. Three counts of intent to distribute, which can carry a prison term of five years to twenty-five years. One count of carrying a firearm, which can carry a prison term of five years to ten years."

I could hear Rob gasping in the background along with the other onlookers in the court. My heart had begun to beat extra fast as the judge shifted his eyes from mine to the sergeant's.

"What were the forensics?" the judge asked the sergeant.

The sergeant stepped forward pulling out a few pieces of paper from his briefcase and placing them in front of the judge before he began to speak.

"This morning at approximately one o'clock a.m., we received a call from an unknown tipster stating that Mr. Jiles, who we have in the courtroom today, and Mr. Bryant Thompson are running a heavy drug ring between the two…"

"And who might the tipster be?" the judge asked, cutting off the sergeant in mid sentence.

"The unknown tipster would like to remain anonymous, Your Honor," said the white sergeant whose face was beginning to turn red at the answer the judge was about to give him.

"Well, Sergeant Silverman, with all due respect, this case cannot proceed unless you reveal the tipster and the allegations," explained the judge.

"Okay, sir, to proceed, the tipster, whose name is Melissa Childs, called in a tip last night to South detectives, stating that the perpetrator—who as I said is present in the courtroom—was Mr. Juan Jiles." He pointed to me as I stood next to him. *No the fuck this bitch didn't lie on Bryant and me. She's gone too far.*

"As the tip came, myself and Detective Barnes handled the report that stated Mr. Jiles and Mr. Thompson were hiding illegal drugs in the Presidential Suites apartment building on Presidential Boulevard in Philadelphia. Once we'd received the tip and had the magistrate sign off on the search warrant, we then executed the warrant and went to the suspect's home where we found three bricks of cocaine, numerous bags of marijuana and a firearm under the bed—a nine-millimeter handgun.

As the sergeant went on with the story my heart fell deeper into the pit of my stomach.

"Plus, Your Honor, when Captain Ingram, along with myself, reached the apartment we found a small brown paper bag sitting on the table that contained small amounts of cocaine, crack rock, and the street term ecstasy pills." I turned around to look at the expression on Rob's face; he seemed flabbergasted. The judge began writing figures down as I stood there with my dick getting hard from the cold air that came in from the vent.

"Okay, Mr. Jiles. Your bail is set at five hundred thousand dollars cash. Are you able to post that today?" He looked at me as if he expected an answer on the spot.

"No, not at this time," I answered.

"Okay, until your bail is paid through a licensed Pennsylvania bail bondsman, you are to be housed at the Philadelphia Federal Correctional Facility." He then banged his gavel on the desk. Almost immediately tears fell from my eyes as the sheriffs took me away into the holding cell. I had never been to jail. I feared for my life. *Someone, please help me.* I closed my eyes and prayed very hard. *God, please help Your child.*

Now I knew who had planted the drugs in my house. *But when did he find the time and how did Melissa know?*

By the time we got to the federal prison all of my tears had dried but I still cried silently on the inside. The blue-and-white school bus pulled inside of a garage known as the intake unit. Me and three other people were shackled together as we walked inside the building. I was led into another holding cell until my name was called to trade my boxer briefs in for a pair of county blues.

After changing into my blues I was given an inmate number which was 981571. I was no longer Juan Jiles. I walked into an area that was known to me as a pod. D-Pod was what they called it. I heard the sounds of people yelling from their cells, TVs and radios blasting.

"We got fresh meat on the block," yelled someone from their cell as I walked up the steps carrying my blanket and sheets in my arms. I couldn't let the other inmates know how scared I was of them and from watching a lot of TV programs I made sure that I would never let a nigga see me sweat.

"Open five cell," yelled the C.O. from the bottom tier. I walked into the cell of two African American young bulls no older than eighteen.

"What's up?" asked the light-skinned dude who wore his hair braided long past his shoulders. The other guy just lay on the top bunk reading a newspaper pretending as if he didn't see me.

"Ayo, what's the deal?" I responded, trying to act hard.

"You can take that bunk right there," the cutie said as I walked over to the bunk to begin making my bed.

"So how long you in here for?" he asked as the other dude turned his face away from the paper. I looked up in his direction and nodded my head to let him know that I noticed him. He nodded back.

"Man, I don't even know. They got me in here on some nut-ass shit," I said. See I could talk that talk when I wanted to. The light-skinned dude walked over to me with an extended arm.

"My name is Dre," he said, now shaking his hand. I put my hand out to shake his. I could tell from the difference in the texture of my skin that we both didn't share the same taste in moisturizing cream.

"I'm Jay," I greeted. I took the liberty of walking over to the other bunk where the other guy was and extended my hand to him as well.

"Just call me J-Rock," he said, shaking my hand with a tight grip. This dude looked much older than eighteen. He was kind of freaky yet not so intimidating. One could compare him to that Philadelphia rapper Freeway. After making my bed I sat there and took in the entire scene. My particular cell was painted light blue with writing on the walls that read—*Bok is a pussy—for a good time call faggot ass Ronny—Keyon was here 2005—me and my bitch* and finally *suck my dick.*

"Chow up," called the C.O. from the bottom tier as all the cell doors began to unlock.

"Yo man, it's time for chow," said J-Rock, hopping down from the top bunk and stepping into his slides. He sported a tight wife beater and county blue bottoms.

"What's chow?" I asked quietly but didn't want to make it obvious that I was naïve.

"That mean it's time to eat, nigga," he responded. Good, because I was hungry anyway. The last thing I remember myself eating was breakfast yesterday morning. We all began to exit the cell. I saw all types of Philadelphians making their way to the chow hall. Some of them I knew from growing up around the way but I made sure not to make eye contact.

Once we got to the chow hall, there was a long line of everyone waiting for their meal. I stood at the tail end holding a plastic cup and a plastic fork. After about ten minutes, I finally reached my turn at the window.

"Ain't you that dude that owns that hair salon on South Street?" said a ghetto, young girl as she gave me my tray. The other inmates that surrounded me started to take heed.

"Who, girl? Let me see who he is because right about now I need me a hairdresser up in this bitch," said a petite girl pushing the other girl out of the way. To my surprise that girl was Miss *Hardcore* herself—Lil' Kim. She looked at me and smiled as she pulled my tray back in to direct the other girl to add more eggs and sausage to my tray.

"You know how to do hair?" she asked standing there with her big brown eyes and of course no makeup with her hair in two braids sporting her county reds. In the federal prison, the women wore red.

"Yes, I own Ché Mystic down in South Philly. What do you know about South Philly?" I asked, taking my tray.

"Chile, since I been in here I learned a lot of Philadelphia. Yo, check it. Can you hook my hair up for me?" I gave her a grizzly look and searched my surroundings. She was asking me if I could do her hair as if we were on the street.

"Kim, how am I gonna do that? We're in jail," I said, switching my body from left to right.

"Nigga, I got pull in this whole muthafuckin' prison. I can do what the fuck I wanna do. Just because I'm locked the fuck up don't make me a slouch. Go 'head and eat your breakfast. I'ma have someone come get you from ya cell in a half hour," she said, talking with her hands as she turned and walked to the back of the kitchen.

I took a seat at the end of the table in the chow hall and ate my breakfast. Thanks to Kim, I had a full meal and I really appreciated it because I was starving.

After leaving the chow hall and before going back to my cell I stopped in the dayroom to use the phone. I had the option of doing that before lockdown. The phones stood on the wall as if they were payphones but they weren't. Everyone had to be called collect. The first call that I made was to my mother.

"Hello," she greeted in her normal weary voice.

"*Bell Atlantic has a collect call from Juan Jiles at the Philadelphia Federal Correctional Facility. To refuse this call, hang up. If you accept this call do not use three-way or call waiting features or you will be disconnected. To accept this call dial one now.*" The phone turned total silent meaning she wished not to accept my call.

The next person that I needed to call was Rob. Fortunately for me he picked up the phone on the first ring and accepted the call.

"Hello," I greeted.

"Girl, what the fuck are you doing with drugs in your house? I am so damn mad at you."

"Damn, Rob, can you cut me some slack. They're not my drugs. My boyfriend planted them there," I said in my defense.

"Well, did *your boyfriend* know that he was gonna get you in this much trouble?" he said in a sarcastic voice.

"Look, Rob, I don't need this shit right now, okay? But I do need your help," I said, changing the subject.

"Well, I may be the employee and you may be my boss, but I'm out here and you're in there so you're gonna listen to me. You have to do something with that ignorant-ass nigga you call a boyfriend. Now whatever you need me to do, I already did it." He stopped me in my tracks.

"Rob, what do you mean, you already did it?"

"I already went to the salon and went through your Rolodex and called your lawyer Mr. Robert Datner, I think his name is?"

"Yes."

"Well, he's already on the case and he'll have you out by tomorrow morning," he said as my heart felt so relieved. I took a deep breath and smiled.

"Thanks, Rob, you know what? I owe you one."

"Yes, you do, girl, and first we're going to start with a raise," he hissed. "Plus, you have a strange message on your voice mail from your former employee Jeff that I think you need to listen to," he added.

"Okay, I'll listen to it first thing when I get home. What I need you to do is make sure everything in the shop is locked up and I'll call you first thing when I get out. Okay?"

"Okay," he responded. I held the phone close to my ear for privacy as the other inmates starting coming back on the block from chow.

"And Rob…"

"Yeah."

"I really appreciate all that you're doing for me. I love you," I said before ending the call. I did that for a reason because I wasn't prepared for what his response was gonna be and I couldn't show my feminine side behind these walls.

"Yo, did you read the paper today?" J-Rock asked Dre.

"Naw, why? What was in there?"

"They talkin' 'bout some bull that owns a hair salon in south Philly. The Po-Po ran up in his crib and took his shit. Man, they said that they found over two hundred fifty thousand dollars' worth of drugs in his crib *and* found a burner underneath his bed."

"Damn, fa' real," said Dre, now lying down on his bunk. "Man, that nigga gonna do some time for that shit." My heart began pumping faster and faster praying that Rob came through like he said he would. I knew he wasn't lying because he said my attorney's name. Rob wouldn't lie about something like that anyway. Besides Anthony, Rob was the closet thing to me.

"Nunber nine-eight-one-five-seven-one, the counselor needs

to see you," yelled the C.O. *What the hell did the counselor want to see me for?* I jumped from my bunk and waited for my cell door to unlock and slide open. As I walked the tier people were staring at me through the slit of their windows watching me walk off the block. I followed the C.O. as he led me to the barbershop area where Kim was sitting in one of the barber chairs. I walked into the air conditioned room as Kim was reading the paper and talking to another female inmate.

"Yo, let me find out that this is your ass up in this paper stashing drugs in your crib. What's that all about?" she asked in her tiny toned voice.

"Yo, that's not my shit, that's my dude's shit," I stated as Kim listened to me closely.

"Well yo, all I'm gonna say is that you better say the right shit in court because if you don't they gonna throw your ass in here like they did me. No, I'm not sayin' snitch on the nigga, just say the right shit," she schooled. I sat down in the barber's chair next to hers.

"Yo, I'm telling you. Those muthafuckin' judges can be shiesty when it comes to handling these nigga cases and they don't play when it comes to perjury. Shit, I'm a living fuckin' example," she continued. "But one thing about me is niggas like to sleep on my shit. Nigga, don't sleep on my shit 'cause when I hit the streets, shit, they gonna hear me comin'. Now what's up with this hair? You gonna fix this shit for me or what, Baby?

"And if I like it, I'ma send you beaucoup clients. I'm talking about major stars in this industry so let's get it rolling." She pointed to the station where she set. "Here's the only shit you can use. You can't use any extension hair."

I looked up on the station to find nothing but hair combs and brushes. But to my surprise, I did find a curling iron.

I combed, brushed, and tucked. I used the curling iron once in a while; I even used the technique that my cousin taught me about using the curling iron to bump the hair. I parted a few strands and clipped others. I laid down a few sides and added some more curls and before she knew it, I was done.

"Oh shit, this is off the chain," said Kim, admiring her do in the mirror. "Ayo, Brandy, come look at this shit." Brandy got up from her seat and walked over to where Kim stood in front of the mirror posing and smiling.

"Damn, I wish he had enough time to do my shit," said Brandy who was sporting two braids as well.

"Thanks, this shit is on point," said Kim now running her fingers through her hair and winking at herself. "What did you say your name was again?"

"My name is Juan and my shop is at Fifteen-thirty-three South Street. Don't forget me, Kim," I said as the C.O. tried to get my attention to take me back to my cell.

"Oh, I'm not. As a matter of fact every time I come to Philly I'm gonna come to ya shop because my hair is bangin'." I gave her two air kisses. "Remember what I said, Baby, you need to look out for you."

"I got it," I said before letting the C.O. take me back to my cell.

The entire tier was dark and there wasn't a sound. I lay on my back stretched out on my bunk when I opened my eyes to Dre standing in front of me still in his boxers holding his long yellow dick in his hand. I wiped my eyes to make sure I wasn't dreaming when I looked up to see J-Rock asleep on his side facing the wall. I lifted my head up from the flat county pillow as Dre slid his sex pole into my warm mouth. I closed my eyes as he began to gyrate his midsection toward the front of my face. I grabbed his thin waist when he began to pump faster.

I made love to his hairy teenage dick as he grabbed the back of my head and started pumping his seven and a half inches into my eating hole. The size of his dick felt good in between my lips as I backed my head up to begin tickling his mushroom head with my tongue. I slid my hand up his wife beater and began fondling his nipple with my thumb and forefinger, letting an erotic force of stimulation shoot through his body. He closed his sexy eyes and tilted his head back as he licked his lips back and forth, then stopping by biting down on his bottom lip.

In the groove, he began to literally fuck my face as my spit mixed in with his pre-cum. I could feel the veins of his sausage pulsate inside my mouth. I ate his dick for breakfast, lunch, and dinner. Through all the stroking and the face fucking, in minutes he exploded his strawberries in my mouth as I swallowed every bit, letting his liquid massage my throat. I licked his dick up and down as it went limp and he tucked it back into his boxers. He turned around and walked over to his bunk to lie down. And I turned over and hugged my flat pillow and went to sleep with a smile on my face.

$$$$$

"Number nine-eight-one-five-seven-one—discharged," the C.O. yelled. I grabbed my flat pillow and my blanket off my bunk, nodded to Dre and J-Rock, and hurried out of the cell. I was given two tokens, a cheap sweat suit and a pair of county slippers to go home in. Instead of going home, I called Rob and had him meet me at the salon.

"Girl, now tell me the tea," said Rob, unlocking the door with his keys because I didn't have mine.

"Well, before I tell you about last night, let me tell you how the fuck I got there in the first place," I said as I quickly went straight back to my office with Rob following behind me.

"I cleaned up what I could from the fight the other day. Everything seems to be working as far as your computer and stuff. I do apologize about that but that bitch had it coming," Rob explained.

"Don't worry about it," I said as I sat down behind my desk and pushed the "play" button on the answering machine. The first message was Jeff.

"Oh, I meant to tell you about that...," said Rob as I put my hand up letting him know to remain silent while I gave my full attention to the message.

"Yeah, y'all bitches thought y'all was doing something when y'all jumped me today but guess what? I got some shit for the both of you. Rob, I'm not done with you yet and Juan, you wonder why your man isn't there for you. It's because he's there for me.

"Yes, I'm fuckin' ya man. You wonder why he never has his jeep is because I am pushing it. I'm the one that he spends his nights with. That's my dick; now what, pussies. Fuck you and your broke-ass shop. That's why it's closing. Yes, I do know everything about you—you fucking crackhead."

Beep.

XI
NO MORE DRAMA

"Damn, before you call me getting all loud and shit, can a nigga get a congratulations?" said Bryant on the other end of the phone. "I just won the custody battle for my daughter."

"First of all, where were you the other night? I waited up for you for hours," I said angrily as I sat back in the chair in my office.

"I had to take care of some business in New York. What the fuck did I tell you about questioning me?"

"Questioning you? Nigga, why the fuck did you stash drugs in my house, Bryant?" I sat up at my desk. The salon was empty except for Rob who was waiting for me in the front.

"What the fuck do you mean 'why'? So the muthafuckin' cops wouldn't get it," he explained.

"Well, Bryant, you were wrong. The cops came to my fuckin' house the other day and took all your shit and I had to go to jail for that shit," I grunted.

"What? Why the fuck did you let them in?"

"Bryant, I had no choice because if I didn't they would have knocked down the fuckin' door. Look, I'm tired of this shit!" I yelled.

"How did they know that I had drugs at your crib?" he asked.

"Because that bitch Melissa went to the cops. And what the fuck are you doing fuckin' with one of my employees?" I had to ask.

"Fuckin' with one of your employees? Who?" he asked, trying to play dumb.

"What the fuck you mean who? Jeff, that's who," I screamed as tears starting falling from my eyes. I began sniffing when Rob came in the office offering me some Kleenex.

"Jeff? C'mon now. I ain't fuckin' with that nigga. That nigga knows my sister and she came home from school to celebrate my birthday. She asked him could he do her hair. Man, I ain't fuckin' with that nigga," he responded. "He sucked my dick a long time ago but I ain't fuck that nigga," he added.

"What the fuck you mean he sucked your dick a long time ago? When I asked you have you ever messed with a dude before, you told me no." I was heated.

"Man, that shit was so long ago I forgot. I ain't fuckin' with dem kats like that. C'mon with that shit. Don't try to play me like I'm some faggot or pussy or something like that cuz it's not going down." He gritted.

"What? See now, Bryant, I am getting sick of your sorry ass. I might have to go to jail because of your shit," I continued to yell as more tears fell.

"Baby, calm down, we're gonna get through this. I'ma get you a lawyer."

"Bryant, I already have a fuckin' lawyer. You got me in some dumb shit that's not even my fault." I sobbed hard as I continued to sit there on the phone.

Rob set an envelope down on my desk as I looked up at him with red eyes. "Look, Juan, I know things can't get any worse but some guys brought this past here the other day. I think you should read it immediately." He then left the room.

"J.J., are you there?" he asked as I ripped the edges of the envelope open.

"Yes, Bryant, I'm here. Since you're so concerned about my well-being, then we both must make an appointment with my lawyer so we can figure this shit out."

"Well, how did you get out of jail?"

"My lawyer got me out on an unsecured bail. I need to take him at least ten grand for him to even start on this case. I'm sure that you will help me raise the money?" I said, still holding the phone close to my ear.

"J, you know I will do all I can for you. I'm sorry that you had to go through that shit alone. I should've played my part and come past the other night when you asked me to. Do you forgive me, boo?" he asked in a lower tone.

"Bryant, I'm hot as shit at you."

"Okay, but check it; my gram is throwing me a victory party tonight at the crib. I want you to swing through."

"Oh, I almost forgot—congratulations!" I said unexcitedly as my eyes rolled in the back of my head. "Oh, I'm finally getting invited to the king's throne, huh?"

"Yes, you are, shawty, and I promise you that I'ma take care of Melissa's ass for once and for all," he said, laughing like it was a fuckin' joke.

"What time is the party?"

"Have ya pretty ass here by seven, so I can chill with you only. Mariah will be gone by then," he stated. If he could've not brought her name up in this conversation it would've worked well with me. "Do you have the address?"

"No, but I'm sure you're gonna get it to me," I said, giving him the grizzly.

"It's five-eight-two-four Chester Avenue. Have ya ass there by midnight, aiight, shawty," he said before the line went dead. I closed my cell phone as I wiped my face from all the tears and the snot that came from my nose. I commenced to open the envelope that Rob had set on my desk. It was a letter from the bank stating that the last rent check had bounced and I must resubmit a check immediately. The balance stood in bold letters at the bottom of the page: $15,238.41.

"Shit," I said out loud as Rob walked into the room. He was dressed casual today wearing a navy blue T-shirt and jeans. He looked stunning compared to my jail sweatsuit.

"Are you okay, girl?" he said, walking around my desk and bending down to give me a hug.

"So you know about this, huh?" I said to him, pointing at the envelope. He walked back around in front of the desk.

"Yes, I must say that I do." He sat down in the chair. We both took a look around the room that was once my luxurious office.

"Do you have it?" he asked blatantly. I looked at him with swollen red eyes.

"You know what, Rob, to tell you the truth, I don't think so," I responded, looking away from him and down to the floor.

"Well, Juan, the first thing is, don't beat yourself up over something that you can't handle. I'm sure that things will fall into place, I'm positive." I continued to stare down at the floor as I began to cry. Rob got up and walked around to grab me with his thick arms while holding my hand and using his free hand to rub my back.

"It'll be okay, come on, Juan. You're a strong person. Don't let this break you down," he said, still rubbing my back. I felt as though my heart could not go on. I needed a break; not merely a break from working but a break from life.

"I don't think I can do this anymore," I said, letting my tears fall onto Rob's shoulder.

"Yes, you can. Don't say that. Juan, as I said before, you're a strong person and if you believe in the man upstairs, then you should know that everything will work out fine. God does not put more on you than you can handle." Rob held me as tight as he could while I let out all my anger and all of my fears.

"It seems like I'm at the end of my rope," I said, sniffling. "I don't know where to turn, my life is so fucked up," I said, continuing to sob. He grabbed my head and held it down on his shoulder.

"It will be okay. Trust me, Juan, it will be okay."

$$\$\$\$\$\$\$$$

I'm young and I'm old—I'm rich and I'm poor—I feel like I've been on this earth many times before. I grooved to the beat of Miss Teena Marie as I drove my car nervously to the Fifty-sixth Street projects to my parents' house. Taking a shower and slipping into my regular clothes made me feel much better. I didn't have any money to waste, so Rob went ahead and opened the shop today while I spent the day off. Unfortunately before I would make my appearance at Bryant's victory party, I thought that I would make a stop to visit my parents.

I slowly pulled into the driveway of the low-income housing buildings and parked on the side of the basketball court where the cuties were sure out running ball and flexing without any shirts on.

"Look at this fuckin' faggot," hissed one of the boys whom I had grown up with. His name was Tyrone and he always stood holding up the wall waiting for customers to come by and buy his dry-ass weed. I gave him a gritty look as I stepped from my

Lexus and slammed the car door. In my arms was a bouquet of red and white roses for my mom and dad and a few *Hype Hair* books that I was featured in. Just something I thought I'd show them to see what I had accomplished.

I walked up the little pathway that led to my parents' back door. I pulled my key out of my pocket and tried using it to open the door. I stuck the key in but for some strange reason it wouldn't turn. I banged on the door.

"Mommy, open the door," I yelled as I looked through the miniblinds she kept at the window. She took her time coming to open the door. She finally opened it wearing a black button-down top and a pair of black slacks with a pair of sandy-brown slippers. She had a surprised look but I couldn't tell if it was a happy surprise look or a what-the-fuck-you-want surprised look. Soon my question would be answered.

"What do you want, Juan?" she said as I walked up to give her a kiss on her cheek.

"Hi, Mommy, I came to see you and Daddy. Is he here?" I asked, handing her the bouquet of flowers. She took them and threw them on the kitchen table.

"Yeah, he's in the living room," she said, closing the door behind her. The house smelled how I remembered it. If the smell of a delicious dinner wasn't seeping through the rooms, you would smell the scent of Pine Sol from my mother always cleaning. But at this particular time, I smelled fried chicken and biscuits.

"Mmm, smells good, Mommy. You must've known that I was coming." I walked into the living room to find my dad in the center of the room laid out in a hospital bed watching Oprah. He turned his weak head to look at me.

"Hi, Daddy," I greeted, walking over to him and planting the back of my hand on his warm cheek. "How are you?"

He didn't say a word; only turned around to finish watching his program. I grabbed onto his hand as he pulled back from mine before he started to speak. He looked up at me with bushy gray eyebrows and wide eyes.

"You ruined this family," he said, trying to talk clearly. My eyes began to water as my mother entered the room.

"Your father is real sick. We don't need you here making things worse," said my mother, taking her seat on the couch.

"Mom, you called *me* and told *me* that Daddy was sick. I came to lend my support and help my father in any way that I can." I turned back around to my father when he had begun to cough up blood. My mother ran over to him after quickly picking up a wipe and a bowl from a nightstand. I backed away and covered my mouth with my hands.

"I never meant to break up our family. I love you, Daddy." I shook my head from side to side letting the tears stream down my face.

"Can't you see you're upsetting him?" I took a seat on the couch and cupped my face in my hands. I never meant to hurt my mother or my father. They would never accept me being gay let alone me opening my own hair salon.

I got up and ran into the kitchen to retrieve the flowers that my mother had tossed on the table.

"Here, Daddy, these are for you." I placed the flowers next to his arm on the bed. He lifted his arm and pushed the flowers onto the floor.

"Juan, get out," my mother said sternly with her back to me as she continued to help with my father. I held my hands over my mouth and began to sob horrendously.

"Mommy," I yelled as I hurried to put my arms around her.

"Get the fuck out!" She pushed me away and pointed toward the door. I stared in her eyes that seemed to be producing fire. I began shaking my head from left to right again.

"Mom, I miss you. I know you miss me. Mommy, please don't do this," I pleaded. I picked up the two *Hype Hair* magazines that lay on the couch and tried handing them to her.

"Mom, look at all I've done with my life. I tried to become something just to please you." My father began to cough again while trying to speak.

"Yeah, you've become something alright. A goddamn sissy," he said still coughing.

"Daddy, no matter what happened between us; I always had love for you," I yelled as I felt a bit of anger entering my soul. "Daddy, you better not lay in this bed and act like you didn't have anything to do with the way I turned out. *You* did this to me!" I yelled with flaring nostrils and a tearful face. The hurt I felt on the inside didn't equal the stinging I felt when my mother smacked me across my face.

My face instantly turned red. "If this is how y'all want it to be, then this is the way it will be. Good-bye," I said before I picked up my magazines and stormed out the door.

I sat in the car in the parking lot and looked through the magazines as my tears started to slow. I looked at all the hairstyles that were not only from my stylists but my own. I'm glad that I had the opportunity to bring closure with my parents. It had almost been ten years of me sending birthday, Mother's Day, and Father's Day cards without getting any response.

I smiled as I flipped through the pages of my accomplishments. *Mommy and Daddy, eat your hearts out*, I thought to myself and sped out of the parking lot and away from Arch Homes.

$$$$$$

I could hear the music as soon as I turned the corner of Fifty-eighth Street. The sounds of Sean Paul filled the rooms of a house that must've been Ms. Bernice's. Before stopping and parking I drove past the house to see if I saw Bryant. There he was standing on the porch holding a paper cup, putting it up to his lips. He turned around to notice me as I got out the car and began to walk toward the front of the house.

"Hol' up, y'all, that's my nigga. I'll be right back," he said, taking a stroll down the steps sporting nothing more than the usual: a wife beater, denim capris, and a pair of black-and-white Air Jordans.

"What's up, Baby?" he asked in a low tone so his boys in the background didn't hear him. I batted my eyes like a cunt.

"I'm good," I said. I was still kind of high from the laced blunt that I'd smoked earlier after leaving my parents' house.

"That's good. I'm glad you could come. Let's find somewhere to park." He hopped into the car as I drove down the street to look for a space. Once he was inside the car he looked around to see if anyone had seen us. He leaned over and kissed me like he owned these lips. I sucked the Budweiser of his tongue as I kissed him some more.

"Here's a parking space," he said, pointing to an empty spot at the corner of the block.

"Damn, my baby got skills," he said referring to me backing into the spot. I smiled.

"I know. My fath…I mean, my uncle taught me how to park before he died," I said, referring to Father Tyrell. We both stepped out of the car in unison.

"Come on, I want you to meet my grandmother," he said excitedly.

"I already met her, remember, when I had to bail your ass out," I teased.

"Oh, yeah, that's right. You did come through for a nigga." We walked down the street to Ms. Bernice's house. I closed my eyes and let the cool air hit my face as my high was beginning to fade away.

"Don't worry, J.J. I got you covered," he said, taking a handful of Ecstasy pills from his pocket. "I'm salty as shit that the cops ran up in your crib and took my shit though, but don't worry. Someone is working on that fa' me."

By the time we got to Ms. Bernice's step everyone had scattered to the inside of the house.

"Ayo, J, my seed is blinded for the rest of her life, man. She's sitting in there with my grams. She vowed to never leave her side," Bryant explained before we walked up the steps and into the house.

The house was extremely decorated to fit this type of occasion. It saddened me to know that Rain would never see this. She would never get the chance to see her father's face again. There were balloons everywhere from the floor to the ceiling, and a lot of people from aunts and uncles to friends and neighbors.

The music played steadily as Bryant introduced me to all his cousins and his nieces and nephews. Of course he introduced me to everybody as his bull. I followed him into the dining room where Ms. Bernice sat at a table wearing a long housecoat bouncing Rain up and down on her knee.

"Hey, Baby," said Ms. Bernice as I greeted her with a kiss on her cheek. Rain laid her head down closely on her great-grandmother's chest with two sterile white gauze pads taped over each eye and two fingers in her mouth. I planted a kiss on her cheek as well.

"Who dat?" she asked, lifting her head from her great-grand-mother's bosom. Ms. Bernice smiled.

"Ohh, Baby, that's a good friend of your daddy's." She placed Rain's head back down as she kissed her forehead and lay her head on top of hers.

"C'mon, let's go into the kitchen," said Bryant as I followed behind him.

"You want a beer?" he asked, digging into a cooler and pulling out a longneck Budweiser before I could respond.

"Sure." I looked around for a bottle opener.

"Here, this is how the real niggas do it." Bryant snatched the bottle from my hand and twisted the cap off with his teeth.

"Gee, thanks," I said as I took my first guzzle.

$$$$$$

"*Rock—steady, steady rockin' all night long,*" sang the Whispers as I later started my fourth bottle of Bud.

"Here, eat this," Bryant demanded as he dropped four pills into my hands. I tossed all the pills into my mouth at once and chased it with my freshly opened bottle of Bud. I bobbed my head to the music as people were walking in and out of the front door giving Bryant and Ms. Bernice their blessings.

"Hey, B, what's up?" said a caramel-complexioned girl as she gave Bryant a hug. She then looked directly into my face. "Hello," she greeted cheerfully. Then she turned her head back toward Bryant as their eyes connected and gave him a nod. He held his beer in the air as if they were sharing a toast. He took a long downer, drinking almost half the bottle, as she walked back into the other room.

"And who was that, might I ask?" I hissed, folding my arms to my chest.

"C'mon, J, that's a girl from up the street. Her and my sister grew up together." I began to get a flashback but all I could see was darkness. The pills were doing something to me. "Haven't I seen her somewhere before?"

My mind became blurry as I tried to think of where I'd seen her but all I could picture was Darnell.

As the people started to leave the party the Ecstasy pills were starting to set in. Ms. Bernice had turned off the music and begun to put the food away in the kitchen.

"You want some orange juice?" Bryant asked.

"Yes, please, I'm very thirsty," I pulled the collar of my shirt because I was starting to get hot.

"Here you go, Baby," said Ms. Bernice as she handed me the glass of O.J. I took the glass and drank the juice at full speed.

"Grandma, I'll take care of this. You can take Rain and go ahead upstairs and get some rest," he said, kissing his grandmother on the cheek.

"Are you sure? I don't want to leave this all for you," she said, preparing to leave the kitchen.

"Yeah, Grandma, I got this and if I need some help I'm sure Loretta will help me when she comes in." A sharp pain shot straight to the front of my head.

"Bryant, I don't think I feel too well," I said, trying to get up from the table.

"Baby, you're gonna be okay. That's just those E pills taking effect," said Bryant walking from the kitchen where Ms. Bernice was.

Ms. Bernice grabbed Rain's hand as they both went upstairs.

The pain in my head became more intense. I stood up and grabbed onto Bryant's shoulder and put my arms around his neck. I was feeling a little faint. That's when someone else grabbed me from behind.

$$$$$$

The room was dark when Greg laid another E pill in between my lips. My dick immediately got hard as Bryant squatted down in front of me and began unbuckling my pants. Greg and I began to kiss passionately like I had never kissed a man before.

He started to suck on my neck as Bryant deep-throated my member in and out of his mouth. I grabbed the back of his head and began to fuck his face as Greg began to lick my nipple while fondling the other. Bryant pulled back from my dick, then began to lick his way around to my man pussy. I bent over like Superhead as he licked in and out of my hole. Greg now took his turn and swallowed my meat like tonight's dinner.

Greg gently laid me down on the kitchen floor as I continued to pump his throat. Man, did this shit feel good. My mind was taken over by two of the sexiest men that had ever walked the streets of Philadelphia. I moaned softly when Bryant began to dip his pole into my mouth. The taste of a hard dick was like heaven. While I dicked the shit out of Greg, Bryant was dicking the shit out of me.

I licked my lips hard because I knew if Greg wouldn't stop eating the shit out of me, then I would soon bust all in his gums.

Greg anxiously lifted me up from the floor and turned me around as I stood on all fours. He forcefully began to penetrate me from the back in a doggy-style position as I continued to suck on Bryant's sausage. Greg smacked my ass cheeks as he entered me from the back. I licked around Bryant's dick and sucked his hair sac like I suck on ice cubes.

"Aww shit," said Bryant as he pulled his muscle from my mouth and busted all over my face. Then he began to massage his cream into my skin with his dick before placing it back into my mouth for me to taste his cherries.

On the other end Greg went to work while tearing up my insides. I could only do but so much moaning while I still had Bryant's member down my throat. He grabbed the back of my head and forced his dick into my mouth and as the head poked my uvula he blew in mid stroke as my jaw locked. Greg then pulled out from behind me and busted his white piss all over my back. I swallowed Bryant's sperm deeply as I let it land in the pit of my stomach and was very appreciative, as Bryant did not only let me have him for this special occasion but his boy, too.

The next morning I woke up to the smell of bacon, eggs, French toast, ham, and whatever else Ms. Bernice was cooking in the kitchen. I lifted my head from the pillow and looked around the room to see posters of naked women, and motorcycles. I also saw steps that led upstairs to the kitchen, which meant that I was in someone's basement. The door opened as Ms. Bernice yelled from the top of the stairs.

"Are y'all hungry?" she asked as Bryant began to squirm, lying on top of the cover in nothing but his boxers and a do-rag.

"Yeah, Grams, we'll be up in a minute," Bryant responded, trying to open his pretty eyes.

"What's up, Baby?" he asked as the insides of my heart melted. I rubbed my hand over his hairy chest. I laid my head down on his chest, noticing his pretty toes that seemed to be hairy as well, like the rest of his fine body.

"Did you have fun last night?" he asked, rubbing my shoulder. "I see you met my little cousin."

"Your little cousin who?"

"Greg! That nigga that you let your back out," he said, leaning over and sparking up a blunt.

"You mean to tell me that I wasn't dreaming?" I asked in shock.

He blew the smoke into my face. "Fuck no, you wasn't dreaming. You let that nigga nut all over your back. I should fuck you up for that shit. I didn't even nut on ya back and you let that punk-ass nigga do some shit like that to you. As a matter of fact, get the fuck out!" he demanded.

I jumped up from the bed. "Bryant, you *can't* be serious," I exclaimed, noticing the anger beginning to run through his blood.

He jumped up from the bed, letting his member fall out from the slit of his boxers.

"Ayo, Grandma, can you close the door?" he hollered upstairs as Ms. Bernice did exactly what she was asked. He stormed closer to me as I jumped back because I really didn't wanna know how it felt to have those flexed fists go upside my head.

"Look, I already fucked him up, don't make me beat ya ass, too."

"But, Bryant, you were fucking me also!" I yelled.

He tightened his lips and balled up his right fist. "Keep ya fuckin' mouth shut, bitch. I was drunk and so was he. I can't believe you let a nigga other than me fuck you in my kitchen." His fist flew across the side of my face, causing me to fall and hit my head on the side of the dresser.

I held my hand over my burning face as he came up to me and kicked me in my ribs.

"Stop!" I yelled as my eyes began to fill up with tears. I couldn't believe what Bryant was doing to me in the basement of his grandmother's home.

"Get the fuck up and get out my house," he said as I lay there in excruciating pain. "Now," he yelled. The basement door opened.

"Bryant Thompson, what's going on down there?" Ms. Bernice asked.

"Nothing, Grandma, I'm just getting a few things off my chest. I'll be up in a minute," he replied without taking his furious eyes off me and flexing his muscles with a closed fist.

"Well, y'all better hurry up before this food gets cold," she said before she slammed the door harder than she did earlier. No one could hear me scream.

He ran over to me in an act to hit me again but stopped in mid swing as I held my hand to cover my face.

"I see you're one of them dumb faggots that will stay with a man at any cost, huh? I could beat you, fuck you, piss on you, and your dumb ass would still be there." He didn't take his eyes off me. "Now this is the last time that I'm gonna say this: Get the fuck out of my house."

"Okay, I'm leaving but please don't hit me no more," I said, getting up and taking my clothes from the arm of the chair. For the last time, he cocked his fist back and this time it landed directly in my eye. I tumbled across the chair and the nightstand from the impact of the blow. I lay there holding my throbbing face and eye. I was trying not to cry because it would make my eye hurt worse.

"What the fuck, you're not listening to me," he grunted as he grabbed the back of my neck and squeezed. I cried out for help but no one could hear me.

"Alright, I'm leaving. I'm leaving," I moaned.

He loosened his grip and stepped away. "Well, get ya shit then." I could feel the whole left side of my face swelling up and there was a lump forming on my head. He watched me like a hawk as I walked around the room grabbing all of my belongings.

"Naw, nigga, put your clothes on. You're not walking through my house like that," he stated with his fist still balled up. As my face swelled, I had to let go to put on my pants and T-shirt. While putting on my shirt I wasn't sure if he was gonna try something else. Before putting on my sneakers, I turned to him.

"Why?" I asked as the burning tears rolled down my face.

He looked me dead in my eyes and responded. "Why not?"

He didn't flinch nor crack a smile. I hurried up the stairs and busted open the basement door to my freedom, or so I thought. Bryant followed.

In the kitchen Ms. Bernice was sitting down having breakfast with Mariah, Rain, and Bryant's sister, Loretta.

"Baby, what happened?" Ms. Bernice asked.

"Grandma, let him go. We got into a fight over some money; that's all," Bryant lied as I walked out the kitchen and then the front door.

XII
I LOVE YOU

The rain poured heavily as I sat and watched from my bedroom window. I hadn't left the house in two days. The salon wasn't making any money due to the bad publicity from newspapers and word of mouth. I definitely wasn't answering any phone calls unless it was one from one of my connects to deliver me some candy.

You would've thought I'd learned my lesson by now but I hadn't. I sat by the window going through the mortgage information on the salon. I had ten days to pay the balance in full or they'd be closing Ché Mystic for good. *Fuck it, maybe I should go be a stylist in a hair salon*, I thought. At least I wouldn't have to put up with the bullshit of paying a fuckin' mortgage. I sat and thought of all the shit I'd been through in the past few months. I got up and walked into the kitchen to get a candle from the drawer.

I lit the candle and sat it in the middle of the coffee table. I bowed my head to say a prayer. I was always taught that if you keep God first, then everything else would work out. And maybe that was my problem all along. I was not keeping God first. I would put God, everybody, and everything above Him. While Darnell lay asleep in his grave I had gone buck wild.

"Buck wild" is a term that I never used when discussing myself. I was always the one to have my shit together. I know that

Father Tyrell was looking down on me right then shaking his head asking, *what the hell is he doing?*

I lit another candle—not for the *death* of Darnell but for the *life* of him. I had waited for him to live his life through me. A man who loved me for who I was and not for what I had or what I was worth. A man who would never put his hands on me or tell me to take drugs. Yes, he may have sparked up a blunt or two but *my* lips never touched one.

I felt tears starting to rise from my tear ducts but I refused to cry another tear. I was gonna hold my head high and live my life like it was meant to be. I lit another candle for my mother and father. There was a time when they were the most important people in my life but now they would be known to me as associates. Associates that I would call my mother and father because they were no longer "Mommy" and "Daddy."

My last and final candle was lit for the life of my baby Anthony. The one person who gave a damn about my well-being. A person whom I could trust hands down. There was no question or doubt in my mind that he wasn't my brother. May God bless him and give him the gift of life just like He gave me. It was my time to shine.

$$$$$$

"I'm not gonna lie to you, Juan. This is gonna be a tough case," said my attorney Robert Datner as he leaned back in his chair and cupped the back of his head with his hands. I had been working with Mr. Datner for some years now. I had hired him when Ieshia and I had gotten into trouble a few years back when we were cashing fraudulent checks. Before Darnell came along, that was how I really had made my money. The term in this gay lifestyle for that type of work was called "crafting."

Now believe it or not crafting was really what it was—crafting. You really needed to learn a skill to portray that type of lifestyle. And if you were a fierce crafter then there wasn't a doubt that you lived FAB. I started off living fab when I earned my first hundred thousand by going to different banks around Philly cashing fraudulent checks. Ieshia and I would cash checks from Philly to Maryland to Richmond. We were unstoppable when it came to the check-writing game.

See, most faggots craft to buy fancy clothes and cell phones and shit. Ieshia and I crafted for money. The *real* money. Money that was used to buy us fancy cars like Beemers and Mercedes-Benzes and shit. But as they say; easy come easy go. We went through that money so quick by buying clothes, jewelry, and cars. And until this day the only thing I had to show for it was my apartment and my car. Now ask me what Ieshia had to show for it—shit.

"I figured that it would be a tough case." I sighed as I looked around his office taking in the scene of pictures of his wife and kids. Robert Datner was one of the best Jewish lawyers that money could buy. He had gotten me and Ieshia off that check-writing shit plus he had gotten my cousin off a murder charge when he used to roll with the JBM (Junior Black Mafia) back in the day.

"Yeah it is. Especially for number one, they found drugs in *your* apartment and number two, there is a key witness that sent them there," he said now looking through his mess of papers on his wooden desk. "Melissa Childs, that's her name," he said as he held the report in his hands.

"So what do I do now?" I asked, trying not to worry about the tremendous jail time I would be facing in the future.

"Well, do you know this girl?"

"Well, I don't *know* her per se, but I do know things about her."

"Well, for this to be so early in the case, I suggest you go to her and talk this out with her so she can't testify at your trial." I was stumped for a minute to think about what he had said. *Me and Melissa talk? No, no,* I thought. *I am gonna kick her ass for spraying mace in my face and stampeding into my shop.* He looked right into my eyes and saw that his suggestion wouldn't work.

"So you're saying that you can't talk to her?"

"I don't think so," I responded, slumping down in the chair.

"Well, like I said, this is still early in the case and the trial will not begin for a few months. We have numerous options to explore. Such as what gave the police probable cause to come search your apartment? Just because they got a tip from some ghetto chick, that's not enough for a warrant from where I stand."

See, that's what I liked about Mr. Datner; he always knew what to do and that is why I wouldn't mind paying top dollar for his services. I stood up from my seat as my cell phone rang. I looked at the number, recognizing that it was my mother and rejected the call.

"Well, thank you for taking time out of your busy schedule and seeing me. And I would also like to thank you for getting my ass out of jail so soon."

"Oh, it was nothing," he said, flagging his hand away. I will help you in any way that I can." He extended his arm for a handshake.

"I will call you when I get some new news about your case. But for now lay low for a while and try not to get into any trouble," he said to me before I walked out of the door.

While walking to my car I heard my cell ring again and it was my mother calling for a second time. *What the hell is she calling me for?* I thought as I opened the phone and closed it. I didn't have anything to say to her after the way she had treated me the other day. I stopped at the pretzel stand a few steps away from Mr. Datner's office and brought me a pretzel with light salt smothered in mustard and a large cherry ice—my all-time childhood favorite.

I took one bite of the pretzel as I started to get a weird feeling in the pit of my stomach. I began to have flashbacks of Darnell lying there in my arms with blood leaking from his nose. I carried the water ice in one hand, my pretzel in the other and it felt like I was holding Darnell in both of my arms. My cell phone rang for a third time but by me carrying these two items to my car, I couldn't reach for it to see who it was.

By the time I got to my car my cell phone had stopped ringing. I jumped in the driver's seat when a voice entered into my head. It was my voice saying good-bye. It was my voice in the same exact tone that I'd used to tell my parents good-bye the other day when I walked out of their house. I licked the top of my water as the voice still flowed through my head and into my ears. *Good-bye…good-bye…good-bye* was all I heard and then a vision of my father appeared in the passenger seat. In an instant, he went away when my cell phone rang a fourth time. This time I looked down at the phone and it seemed like I heard my mother's voice in my head screaming, *Juan, you better answer this damn phone.* I flicked open the phone and held it to my ear for a second before saying hello.

"Mom," I answered.

"Juan, you were the first person I wanted to call. Your father passed away about ten minutes ago," she informed me as she wept. I sat in the driver's seat in silence, letting the water ice drip down onto my hands. My eyes swelled up with tears.

"Mommy?" I cried.

"Yes, Juan."

"I'm on my way."

"Okay," she responded before I closed my phone.

More and more tears started to fall as I got closer to West Philadelphia and the Arch Homes. I glanced in the rearview mirror thinking of an explanation to tell my mother about how my face had gotten like this. The closer I drove to the streets of my childhood the memories started flooding.

There was the time when my father had taught me how to ride a bike along with the time when he first took the training wheels off. I rode past Fifty-fifth Street where we used to light firecrackers on the Fourth of July. Apple Tree Street, hmmm; that's the block where my father came and got me out of a house party that took place at two in the morning.

The field across the street, which was now turned into a nursing home, was where I'd first played the game "Catch a Girl, Freak a Girl."

The Salvation Army; now that was my spot back in the day. I would go there every day for the after-school programs. Then by the time I was old enough, I would go to the gym and sit in the bleachers and watch the boys play basketball. I always had my eyes on this one particular boy named Terrance. He was a lot older than me but he was fine as hell. I loved the way he'd run up and down the court grabbing the ball and shooting it into the net. He moved away when I was sixteen and I hadn't seen him since.

By the time I got to the projects, the ambulance was taking

my father away. I pulled up in the driveway and got out, passing by the onlookers who were trying to find out what they could see.

"I'm sorry to hear about your father," said a skinny, dark-skinned lady who used to babysit me when I was younger. She was now known as a babysitter-turned-crackhead. *What am I saying? Like I got room to talk.*

My mother stood in the doorway as the ambulance rode slowly down Vodgers Street.

"Mommy," I cried, running into her arms as she welcomed me. I squeezed her flesh as tight as I could, trying not to let her go as she did the same. We both held each other and cried. I cried for good reasons and bad.

"I'm so sorry," she said, holding me tighter as tears fell from her eyes.

"Mom, no! It's not your fault." Only if my mother knew all the hurt and pain that I felt on the inside. I missed my family so much that I couldn't breathe. She pulled away from me with red eyes.

"Your father loved you. He always loved you," she said, wiping my tears away with her thumbs. I grabbed her again as we held each other tight and let the nature of a death in our family take its course.

$$$$$

"Thanks for everything," said a female client as she paid me for her do as well as gave me a ten-dollar tip.

"You're welcome. I'll see you in two weeks?" I asked, knowing that her curls would fall in one.

"Yup," she responded walking out the door. Rob was finishing up one client's hair when he walked over to me.

"Are you okay, girl?" he asked, still holding a styling comb in his hand.

"Yeah, I'm fine. How about you?"

"I'm doing well. Your face is healing well. How's your mother doing? Are y'all done making the funeral arrangements?"

"No, we still have a little more prepping to do. Everything will be done by Wednesday," I said, walking back into my office.

"Oh, okay, so that's when the funeral is, huh? Where is it gonna be?"

"It's gonna be at my grandmother's church; Liberty Baptist on Fifty-seventh and Larchwood." I went into my office, sat behind my desk and started up my computer. I hadn't checked my email in quite some time. I signed on to AOL and I had over a hundred emails. Most of them were junk emails but two were from Bryant.

My first instinct was to delete the email but then I decided to read it only to hear what he had to say. I opened it to see that it was a poem written yesterday.

Listen to my words as I say that everything's gonna be OK
Sometimes you might have a bad day but know,
everything's gonna be OK
Your day might not be going too good and you wish
you were home, around the hood
Laughing and joking with your love thinking everything
was all good
To make the time go by, do what you gotta do
Cuz, boy, you know ya man is here, sitting here waiting on you

To hold, to love, to pamper, cuz I know the loss of
your father can be a damper
Know that ya man loves you in the worst way and when you say
I can come home, I'll make you forget about your bad day
So finish up at work and forget about your bad day
Listen when ya man says everything's gonna be OK

I deleted the email and then deleted the poem. But the other email, I read carefully as his thoughts and emotions filled the entire room.

Dear Juan, my one and only J.J.,

How could I sit here and write this letter to you knowing all the bad things I've done to you. My soul is burning not having you around. At this point in my life I realized that I need you so much. I know that you might not read this letter because of the way I played you but, Baby, if you can find it in your heart to forgive me, I promise that I will make it up to you. Right now, I'm not thinking of anyone else but you. Baby, I need you in my life. Fuck dem other hoes out there. This is one man that only wants to be with you.

Listen, I know I was on some psycho shit the other day when I hurt you but you must know that I swear to Allah that I didn't mean that. If you forgive me then it's all about me and you. Mariah miscarried my seed so there's no reason for me to keep her around. I will come out of the closet for you. Baby, please give me another chance. If you love me the way you say that you do, then you will meet me tonight at Zanzibar Blue at 7:00 p.m. sharp. I love you, boo.

Love Always,
Bryant

I lowered my head with my eyes piercing the floor. This letter was unexpected and I vowed to myself to get rid of Bryant and all his dumb shit for good. *Why would he do this? If he says he loves me as much as he says, then he should allow me to go my way,* I thought. A knock came upon the door as I quickly fixed my face to communicate with whomever it was.

"Who is it?" I said, fixing up the papers on my desk to look as if I were very busy.

"Juan, it's me Keisha and my sister Kya. Can we speak with you for a moment?" I pushed all the papers into a pile and stuffed them in my desk drawer.

"Sure, come in," I responded, now pulling my hair back into a rubber band not caring how badly bruised they thought my face. They both walked into my office, one behind another, wearing matching flaring skirts and sandals from Express. They sat down in the chairs on the opposite side on my desk.

"What's up?" I asked, putting my elbows on the desk and holding my head down with folded hands. They both looked at each other with Kya sporting a burgundy wrap and Keisha sporting a wet and wavy.

"You wanna go first or should I go first?" asked Keisha, moving her index finger between the two.

"You go first," said Kya. Keisha looked at me and took a deep breath.

"Okay, Juan, I'm gonna tell it to you like this. We're not happy here and we're taking the job next door at Chez Sonia's." She watched my every move to see my reaction.

"Okay, why aren't you happy?" I asked, giving them my undivided attention.

"Well, first of all, when we started everything was okay. Now,

I don't mean to be in ya business or anything but now it seems like this shop is going under. We're not making any money due to poor clientele. The police are always busting up in here for something and that's another thing. We don't feel safe," she said, shaking her head from side to side. I continued to sit while Kya decided to speak.

"Yes, Juan, we don't want you to feel like we're betraying you or anything but we have rent to pay and since you went up on the rent here, we're not making enough." I shifted my eyes between the both of them as they took turns speaking.

"I mean, there's no toilet paper in the bathrooms anymore. There are no supplies to work with. As employees of this salon we feel that you owe it to us to let us know what's going on," Keisha added. I moved forward in my seat to begin to address their concerns.

"Well, Keisha, I wished you would have come to me first before taking a job next door. And it's not my fault if my employees want to fight each other."

"What do you mean it's not your fault? It is your fault to have girls running up in here fighting us over some nigga," Keisha said, getting hyped.

"Keisha, I'ma need to you to calm your voice in *my* salon." I stated firmly.

"Calm my voice, pussy, I'm mad as shit 'cause I'm still working here without gettin' paid and my jaw still hasn't been the same since that girl that your boyfriend is fucking punched me for no reason. I didn't have anything to do with that shit," she continued in a loud tone.

"Look, y'all, did ya'll come in here to argue with me or talk to me?"

"We came in here to talk and now we're talkin' so what are you gonna do to change things?" Keisha said abruptly. I took another deep breath because honestly, I didn't know how to handle this. I stood up from my seat.

"Rob, could you come in here for a second?" I yelled. Keisha turned around toward Kya and then back to me.

"And what the fuck is he supposed to do?"

"He is the manager of this salon and I feel it's only right that he listen to your concerns." Rob came into the office.

"Yes," he said, still holding onto the doorknob.

"Rob, our stylists say that they're not happy here due to the lack of funds around here lately. Keshia says she doesn't feel safe. I don't know what to do," I said, plopping back down into my chair.

"Well, the only thing that I can say is that right now Ché Mystic is having a little financial trouble and if y'all are willing to stay and hold on until things get better, then you're more than welcome to stay. If not, I'm sorry." Rob covered it all in a nutshell.

Keisha stood from her seat and slammed her hand down on my desk. Well…

The front door of the salon swung open so hard it hit the wall and the glass broke. My heart fell, ruining the lining of my stomach.

"Rob, where the fuck are you?" Jeff yelled as he entered the shop with four boys following behind him. Keshia jumped back toward the wall as Rob tried to run behind my desk.

"What the fuck are you doing here?" I yelled to Jeff as the other boys came toward me.

"Where's all your money?" asked one of the boys wearing a

black Dickie set. Actually all of them had on black Dickies except for Jeff.

"No, fuck the money, I want him," yelled Jeff, pointing to Rob with a twelve-inch sharp blade.

"Boy, you better not stab me with that knife," yelled Rob. Keisha and Kya ran out of the office as all four boys ran toward me and Rob. I turned and tried to run as I tripped over a stack of magazines I had sitting beside my desk. The four boys grabbed Rob and pinned him to the floor as Jeff began punching and kicking him in his stomach.

One of the boys grabbed Rob by the head and began jabbing him in the mouth as Jeff took his sharpie toward Rob's throat and deeply slit it from right to left. I screamed to the top of my lungs as Rob's blood gushed from his skin as one of the boys let his lifeless head go and made a thump sound as it hit the floor. The four boys ran out of the shop one right behind the other with Jeff tailing behind.

Rob lay on my office floor with his legs twisted and his arms spread out. His eyes were closed as if he were asleep.

"Noooo," I screamed as I ran throughout the shop looking for Keshia and Kya but they had vanished and so had Jeff and all his boys.

$$$$$$

The sun had begun to set as the police did their last walk-through of the salon making sure they had all the evidence needed to look for Rob's killer. I cringed at the thought of Rob being dead. The look of his chocolate face lying there in my office in a pool of blood will always scare me.

The smell of blood throughout the salon freaked me out. I was traumatized from what I had seen. I needed to be comforted, I needed to be saved and not the type of saving that comes from a man. I'm talking about the type of saving that only God can give me.

Through all the blood and fingerprint dust and police tape, I got down on my knees and prayed to the Lord for forgiveness for all I had done. This shop was going down like the Titanic and the Lord was gonna let it sink. Maybe it was meant to be. I needed to be forgiven but then I thought that in order for me to be forgiven then I must first forgive.

$$\$\$\$\$\$$$

The candles that were lit on each table set the mood right as I entered the door of Zanzibar Blue.

"Hi, will you be dining alone or are you here with people?" said the African-American female who greeted me as soon as I walked through the door.

"I'm supposed to be meeting someone here," I responded, noticing Bryant in the distance sporting a black blazer and a Kangol. He motioned for me to come in his direction.

"There he is," I said, walking past the hostess and over to my man.

"Enjoy," she said. As soon as I came within his distance he stood up and we embraced with a four-arm hug. He inhaled my scent the way I'd inhaled his cologne, which was Burberry Brown. I could tell his sincerity by the way he gripped the lower part of my back.

"I'm sorry, Baby," he said as he held me close. I backed away from him and took my seat at the table.

"Let me get that," he said, grabbing the chair and pulling it from the table so I could sit.

"Thanks," I said as he helped push me toward the table. "So, Bryant, what's this all about?" I asked, cutting to the chase. My father was being buried tomorrow and I had no time for games.

"J.J., I brought you here tonight because I wanted to show you how much I missed you the past couple of days. Baby, what happened at my grandmother's house the other morning, Baby, that wasn't me." His eyes started to tear up through the flames of the candles.

"Bryant, I might be going to jail because of you," I hissed as his tears made an appearance. For the first time in my life; I had seen a thug cry.

"Baby, no you won't," he protested.

"Yes, I will, if she testifies against me, I will."

"Baby, no, you won't," he spat, now bawling out of control.

"What makes you so sure?"

"Because she's dead," he said as my eyes widened with surprise. The waitress came over to our table.

"Can I start you two off with a few drinks?" she asked cheerfully. Bryant looked up at her with his teary eyes. She read him like a book. "I'll give you some time. I'll be back."

"Bryant, what the hell you mean, she's dead? What the hell happened?" I asked, trying not to let anyone hear our conversation.

His tears began to fall steadily as he told his story for the first time.

"I had her murdered, J." He put his hands on top of the table as I placed my hand in his. "I did it," he said, now with snot running from his nose. He squeezed my hand causing my fist to ball.

"Bryant, stop crying and tell me what happened," I demanded. He took a few sniffles, then blew his nose with the napkin and prepared himself to tell me the full story.

"That bitch blinded my daughter for life, yo. Then she had the nerve to kill my seed and send me the pictures. I offed that bitch," he spat in anger. He straightened his face and got himself together. "My bad, shawty, I just needed to get that out. I'm ready to order now." He called the waitress over to our table.

"Bryant, we need to talk." I stopped the waitress in mid sentence before she started telling us what the day's specials were.

"Okay, I guess I'll give y'all a little more time," she said as she spun a one-eighty in the other direction.

"Baby, you wanna talk, then let's talk. Like I said in my email, I'm all *for* you." he said, talking with his hands. "What is it that you wanna talk about?" I took a sip of the ice water from the table.

"We need to talk about us. Bryant, I need more than what you're willing to give me. I need more than a piece of dick. I need a man, a companion. Someone that's gonna be there in my time of need."

"I feel you," he said, nodding his head in agreeance. "So basically you're telling me that you want *me* to be your man?"

"Bryant, I'm not *telling* you anything. If you choose to be with me and stop all the lies and commit to me, then fine, but if you can't, then you need to step," I said, looking him dead in his eyes. "And look at me; you basically turned me into a crack-head. I had never thought about taking drugs until *you* came into my life."

He looked down at the flowery prints on the table. He then looked up.

"Baby, the drugs are going to stop. I promise you I will get a real job only if you give me the time. Anything you need from me—you have it. Rehab, time to yourself—Baby, you got it. Just put in a little bit of faith, J.J." We both stood silent as the music from the jazz band played on.

"Listen, Baby, I love you and I would do anything in this world for you. You saw that I took care of Melissa; not just because of what she did to my daughter but for what she's done to you."

The waitress came back to the table. "Oh, are we smiling now," she said jokingly. "May I now take your orders?"

Bryant looked at me with a sexy smirk on his face. "Baby, you order first."

"Okay." I briefly looked over the menu. "I'll have the stuffed duck with a side of orange rice and cabbage." I closed the menu and looked in his direction. "And what will you have, honey?," I said in a way to see his reaction. He shocked the hell out of me when he seemed not to mind that I had called him out in public. He looked over the menu himself as he palmed his hands underneath the table.

"I'll have the roast chicken with mashed potatoes and gravy," he said, closing his menu and handing it back to her. "We will also have two glasses of your finest wine," he added without taking his eyes off me.

"Okay, I'll take your menus and be right back with your drinks." The waitress smiled. The mood got quite silent for a minute before he began to speak.

"J.J., I need to say this. You're the most honest, beautiful, and most considerate person I've ever met. I'm truly sorry for ever laying a hand on you the other day. And not to offend you by any means but even with a bruised face, you're still beautiful," He glimmered as his eyes matched my soul. I smiled at his lovely demeanor.

"Well, Bryant, I can honestly say that this morning, I hated you. But after seeing one of my friends get murdered today, it made me think about life and how short it is. And there is no time to walk around holding a grudge against someone that I truly loved. I had to realize that the person I love is you." I held my head high as I spilled my guts to the man who would in the future make me happy.

"You know, J, I'm glad to hear you say that because I want to take our commitment a step further." He smirked.

"A step further; what do you mean by that?" I asked as the waitress came back with our drinks.

"Here you go," she said, setting the glasses of red wine in front of us.

"Thank you," I said before directing my attention back to my b-boy. "Now back to what you were saying. You would like us to move a step further?" I was anxious to know what he meant.

Again his put his hands on top of the table and I placed my hands in his.

"I want us to move in together." He squeezed my hand and smiled. I almost jumped out of my socks. *Does he really mean that he wants us to move in together? Does he realize what he's talking about? If he is to move in my apartment with me then this will definitely be a step in the right direction to making him all mine.*

"Bryant, are you serious?" I asked reassuring that I wasn't dreaming. My eyes were as bright as the sun as the flames from the candles danced back and forth on our tabletop.

"Yes, Baby, I'm serious. I can move today, if need be."

"Bryant, I really do need you in my life right now. I love you and I do forgive you for everything you've done to me." I thought about the prayer I'd said this morning. "Yes, I would love to have your presence in my home."

He squeezed my hands a little harder before letting them go and picking up his glass and holding it out to toast. I picked up my glass by the stem.

"A toast."

"A toast," I said, repeating after him and smiling.

"To a new beginning of us," he said. We both let our glasses clink as we held them to our mouths and swallowed slowly. This was the first time I could say that I was in love or might I say *we* were in love.

$$\$\$\$\$\$\$$$

"Sir, please hold up a minute," said Bryant as he ran behind a man selling flowers on the corner of Conshohocken and City Avenue. He slipped the guy a twenty and the guy gave him a dozen red roses.

"My queen," he said as he handed me the roses.

"Aww, Bryant. Thank you, I love you so much. Now gimme a kiss," I said as he looked around a few times, then planted a soft kiss on my lips.

"Man, you gon' get me killed out here," he said as we began to walk faster to my apartment.

"Bryant, it's dark out here and plus, ain't nobody worried about us this time of the night." We walked in the vestibule of my apartment building.

"Good evening, Trudy," I said, holding on to Bryant's arm and trying to carry the roses at the same time.

"Good evening, Mr. Jiles. How are you this evening?" she

asked, holding her earpiece in her ear as she stood behind the clerk's desk.

"I'm fine now. Can you hold any visitors for me tonight and I'll be putting the DO NOT DISTURB button on my telephone, so please take all my calls. Thanks."

"Will do," she said, getting right down to business by typing my information into the computer.

"Damn, that's one bad-ass Asian chick," Bryant said, giggling as we got onto the elevator.

"Shut up! I'm the only person you should be looking at," I said, giving him a great kiss, tasting his delicious tongue. We kissed and grinded all the way to my floor. I could have sworn I felt his dick jump when the elevator beeped.

"Look at you. You're so damn drunk that you can't even get the key into the knob. Here, let me get it for you," he said, moving me to the side so he could open the door. Those martinis I had at dinner, plus the bump, really had me feeling fine.

Soon as we entered the apartment, without even turning on the lights, I threw the bouquet of flowers on the floor and I went down with them dropping straight to my knees. I couldn't wait to taste his big daddy in my mouth. As soon as I unzipped his jeans his dick was already out of his boxers. All I had to do was insert it into my warm, liquored-down mouth. I closed my eyes as I took all of him in without him even budging for me to stop. In fact he lifted his T-shirt so I could get a good suck as he pushed the back of my head into him. His dick smelled sweaty and musky and I loved it. I would call it a sports dick because it smelled like he played sports. He grabbed both of my ears as he fucked my face so hard that he busted all in my grill.

I swallowed his ice cream whole as we began kissing again and taking off all our clothes and walked slowly toward the bedroom. I made a mistake and kicked the Jesus nightlight from the socket as we eased down the hallway and into my room where we intertwined and fell on the bed.

"Baby, I want you," he said in a seductive tone.

"I want you too," I agreed. He sucked on his bottom lip and began kissing me again.

"Naw, I'm saying, I want you. Meaning, I want you inside *me* tonight." I was so distraught at what he'd said because the thought had never crossed my mind that I was gonna fuck *my* man.

"You want *me* to fuck you?" I asked for assurance. He looked at me with his bedroom eyes and began to suck on his bottom lip again.

"Yeah, Baby, what's wrong with that?" he asked as he began to massage my waistline.

"Nothing. I mean there's nothing wrong with that." I started kissing him as my whole feminine demeanor changed now that I was the top. I kissed him hard as I licked all over his lips while massaging his ass cheeks getting me prepared to enter the dark tunnel of love.

I turned him around and laid him down on the bed, then went over to my dresser where I kept my KY Jelly.

"Put dat ass in the air," I said as I poured the jelly on my dick and rubbed some on his hairy anus. The one thing about Bryant's ass was that it was perfectly round and ready to be stuck. I moved his body toward my torso so I could fuck him doggy style while I stood with my knees touching the bed. I used my strength to pull his body forward as I smoothly stuck my dick in his rectum.

I tried to look at the expression on his face from behind to see if he'd ever done this before but I couldn't. I then pulled out as his eyes opened.

"What the fuck is up?" he yelled.

"Chill," I said. "I'm gonna look for a CD to groove to while I'm tearing that ass up," I continued. I walked around the room with my dick hard as a rock. With every step I made sure that I stroked it so it wouldn't get soft by default. I looked at my CD collection and passed by TLC, India Arie, Chaka Khan, and then stopped at Johnny Gill.

I pulled the disc from the holder and inserted it into the disc player and pressed *random*. The first song that started to play was a "Quiet Time to Play." I walked back over to the bed where Bryant was ass naked posted on all fours.

"Are you ready for wifey?" I said, rubbing my finger up and down his asshole preparing to finger-fuck him. I slipped my finger in his anus and pushed it all the way in until I couldn't go no farther. Then I replaced my finger with my hard dick.

I slowly pushed myself in as his face cringed a little. But when I pulled it out, he seemed to have exhaled. I pushed it back in, then began pumping to the beat of the song.

"*Ahh shit*," he moaned as I pumped to the rhythm. I grabbed his bubble butt and started long-stroking him as if I was in charge. Now I knew the true meaning of "a pancake ain't done unless you flip it" or "the chicken ain't done unless you cook it on both sides."

"Damn, boy, that feels good," he said as he began jerking his dick while I pumped his ass harder. I knew that it was starting to feel good to him when he started to throw that ass back to me. I closed my eyes and began fucking the shit out of him. I began thinking all the things that a thug stood for. I was fucking a nigga with a head full of cornrows to the back. The same nigga that stood posted up on your corner selling that shit. He moaned seductively as I stroked my pipe in and out his wet-ass thug style. Yes, I was getting ass straight up from the same nigga that had baby moms out there in the streets that were in love with them. They would never know that I had their man doggy style. Mariah would never think of a day when her man was getting fucked in the ass.

"Do you want me to stop?" I said as the sweat beads formed on my forehead with Johnny pouring his heart out in the background.

"Naw, nigga, keep going. I'ma bout to nut," he said as I flipped him over, pushed him up on the bed and raised his legs putting one over each shoulder. I was in it. I was tearing up those thug guts.

"Shit, J.J., I didn't know that it would be like this," he said while catching his breath. I looked him in his eyes as I pumped faster.

"You want me?" I said with sweat pouring down my face. He held his eyes shut tight as I tore up his insides just like he did mine.

"Huh?"

"I said do you want me? You heard what I said." I was trying to sound dominant.

"Yeah, J.J, I want you," he moaned as I knew he could feel me in his stomach. I leaned over and kissed his lips and kissed him hard until my bust and cream coated his entire stomach.

While I lay on top of his chest after our escapade, I definitely knew that I was in love with my thug.

XIII
NEGATIVE VS. POSITIVE

The butterflies in the pit of my stomach got worse as the limo pulled up in front of my parents' door. The family decided to wear white, a symbol of purity, rather than black to seem dark and gloomy.

All of my aunts, uncles, and cousins had come in from out of town to share this house full of food. The smell of turkey, chicken, collard greens, sweet potatoes, and mac and cheese filled my nose as I sat in the kitchen rocking back and forth from nervousness.

"Juan, Baby, you got so big. Stand up and give your Aunt Ada some sugar," she said, extending her arms out to me to hug her. As she kissed the side of my face I could smell that she had overdone it on the perfume. "Stand back and let me take a look at you. I saw you in one of those magazines. Your momma must be real proud," she stated, looking over to my mother who smiled and agreed with her. "Do you still own your own shop?"

"Yes."

"Hmm, I need to come down there and get something done to my hair," she said, patting her hand on top of her head where her wig sat.

"Okay, y'all come on now. The car is outside," said one of my boy cousins walking into the kitchen sporting a cream suit similar to the linen suit that I wore. I stood up and my mother came over to me.

"Mom, I don't think I should go," I said, shaking my head when my Aunt Ada overheard me.

"Yes, you have to go," Aunt Ada snapped. "Because if you don't then you're gonna regret not having closure. You will start to have bad dreams and they will never go away. Now you love your father, don't you?"

"Yes," I responded as a lonely tear fell from my eye and down my cheek.

"Well, let's go say good-bye to your father." She grabbed my hand and led me into the living room with my mother tailing behind rubbing my back.

The living room was crowded with my family from both sides. My uncles sat on the couch as they discussed the Eagles game that had aired last week while my little cousin sat talking about boys.

I walked on the porch where the neighbors were waiting for my mother to come out. Half the project was out looking, waiting for my family to make an entrance into the limo.

"How are you feeling?" asked my little homie Rondell standing with a basketball in his hand. Rondell and I were the best of friends while growing up. I was his big brother when I'd volunteered for the Big Brothers and Big Sisters program of Philadelphia. But by the time he turned eighteen he'd gone off to college on a basketball scholarship and now some bigwigs up in New York were having talks about him being drafted to the NBA. He was now twenty-one. We hugged and gave each other dap.

"I'm fine for right now," I said. "But I really don't wanna go to the funeral," I added.

"How are you not gonna go to your own father's funeral?" he asked, bouncing the basketball.

"Because, Rondell, I can't imagine my father lying in a casket. I thought I would at least be in my forties or fifties when either of my parents died but I'm in my twenties and this shit don't feel right."

He turned to face me as he held the basketball in his arm. "Look, when my grandmother died, I didn't know what I was gonna do. I didn't know where to turn but I knew I needed to be strong for my mother. Just pray and know that things are gonna work out. Remember! That's what you used to always tell me."

I looked at him and smiled. One thing I can say about Rondell is that he always knew what to say to make me feel better.

"You know what, baby boy, you're right." I looked at him and smiled. "So you do listen when I talk to you, huh?" I teased.

"Well, someone has to keep you on your toes," he said as he gave me a long hug. "Now go ahead with your family to your father's funeral and act like the fuck you know," he demanded.

"Nigga, don't be cursing at me. Sometimes you forget that I'm *your* big brother," I said.

"No, I'm *your* big brother," he teased as he began bouncing the basketball.

"Go ahead, dude, I'll check you later."

"Alright, Rondell."

"One."

"Juan, come into the house so we can have prayer," yelled my Uncle Lewis from the doorway. I ran back into the house so I could say a prayer of comfort for me and my family.

The ride to the church was as dreadful as watching Rob lie on my office floor having his life slip away. One of my aunts had forgotten her bottled water in the house so that gave me more reason to stall.

The front of the church was decked out in wreaths and flags and there were a lot of people waiting for our arrival—mostly distant family and friends who had begun to line up outside the church. The driver got out of the limo and walked around to let my mother and me out first.

I don't wanna go, I thought to myself with my eyes filling up with tears. I grabbed a hold to my cousin Nicole's hand as I screamed to the top of my lungs.

"I don't wanna go in there," I yelled with tears falling down my face. My mother stood in front of me, holding on to my uncle as the funeral director led us up the red steps and into the church. Everyone was at peace with the fact that my father had been sick but it still hadn't set into my mind. My tears were falling as we two stepped into the church as the director recited the "Lord's Prayer."

My legs felt so weak, I couldn't stand. Another cousin, Mona, stood on the other side of me and we slowly walked into the church. I looked up through blurry eyes to see the flowers that lay on top of the open casket. I couldn't do this. This was one funeral that I was not ready for. The closer we got to the casket the more tears fell from my eyes.

"Oh my God," I yelled as the rest of the people in the church looked on. By the time my mother got to the casket I began to fall down. I saw my mother bend down to kiss a man on his fore-head and that man was my father.

The funeral director motioned to my cousin and me that we were next. Somehow I was able let go of both of my cousin's hands. I turned and hightailed out of the church. I ran through the crowd—out of the door and down the steps skipping two at a time with Mona, Nicole, and Bryant running behind me. I got to the bottom of the steps and screamed loud as I thought of my father teaching me how to climb trees, sitting me on his lap while driving in a car and, most of all, telling me to kiss his cheek every morning before school.

I just couldn't do it. I could not go back into that church. I sobbed, lying my head down on Nicole's double D's after she'd caught up with me.

"Calm down. Everything is gonna be alright," she said, running her hands through my hair.

"Look, Bryant and Mona are here with you. We're all gonna go in there together," said Nicole, grabbing my hand and walking with me slowly up the steps and back into the church. I grabbed her hand and squeezed as tight as I could as my Aunt Lucy grabbed my other hand. I sobbed loudly all the way to the front of the church. I passed by all my family members that sat on one side of the church while my dad's neighbors and family and friends sat on the other.

I regretted this day from the bottom of my heart. I loved my father very much, no matter what he'd done or said to me in the past. My heart felt heavy as I approached the tan-colored casket looking at my dad lying in a brown suit. His eyes were closed tight and his hands were folded very neatly over his stomach.

"See, your dad is at peace," said Nicole as she held me up by the lower part of my back. "He's at peace now. Here, touch him."

My face was wet from tears, sweat, and snot. I held my hand out to touch his cheek. I fixed his tie that seemed to be a little crooked. I looked down at his shoes to make sure they matched his suit. My daddy was lying there dead. I looked up to the ceiling of the church.

"Oh, God, I can't breathe," I yelled as Bryant, Mona, and Nicole walked me over to a seat next to my mother who was being comforted by her brother, my Uncle Lewis. I laid my head down on Nicole's shoulder and the choir began to sing as the ushers passed out the programs.

I looked down at my dad's picture on the front and thought, *this can't be.* The tears would not stop. One of the ushers handed Nicole a Kleenex and she handed it to me to dab my eyes. *Oh, God, why my daddy?* were the words that flowed through my mind. After about twenty minutes my eyes cleared up as I had come to realize that I should not question where God puts a period.

$$\$\$\$\$\$\$$$

"So I know you're happy that you're going home today," I said to Anthony as I helped him pack his bag while we waited for his discharge papers.

"You're damn right I'm happy. I'm tired of lying in this bed all day and I'm tired of eating this hospital food," he joked, trying to get up from the bed but needing help. Since Anthony had been in the hospital he had lost a lot of weight and his bones were quite frail.

"Here, let me help you," I said, helping him from the bed into the wheelchair. He looked up into my eyes after he'd sat down.

"You know, I'm so sorry to hear of your dad and your friend passing."

"Thank you," I said, getting him together. "That's okay, Anthony, because both of them are in a better place now." I reached over for the remote to turn off the TV.

Knock, knock.

"Come in," said Anthony in a weak tone. A young Caucasian lady with long, jet-black hair entered the room wearing a long white lab coat.

"Hey! How are you today?" she said, squatting down to Anthony's eye level.

"I'm fine, just happy to be going home," Anthony responded cheerfully. I sat on the side of the bed waiting for the doctor to hand Anthony the discharge papers for him to sign.

"Yeah, I know you are but here's the thing. Um, I need to speak with you about something very important," she said in a low tone.

"Sure, what's up?" Anthony shot back excitedly. I made myself comfortable on the bed because I had a feeling that this was gonna be a long drawn-out discussion on how he needed to take care of his new kidney once he was released.

"Um, it's kind of personal. Do you wish to have someone in the room while I talk to you or would you like us to talk in private," she said, looking over at me and then at him. Anthony turned to me with a smile on his face.

"Juan, can you please step out of the room for a minute while I talk to the doctor?"

"Sure," I said, getting up from the bed and setting his bags down. "I'll be right out in the hall if you need me."

"Okay, love you," Anthony said.

"Love you back." I walked out the door closing it behind me.

I walked around to the snack machine and bought a bag of my favorite candy, M&M's with almonds. Ohhh, I loved them. By the time I got back around to Anthony's room I heard a loud scream.

"Aaaahhhh," yelled Anthony from inside the room. I knocked

on the door before opening it and walking in. Anthony was now in a wheelchair and screaming hysterically.

"Can you please stand outside?" the doctor asked as I tried my hardest to follow her orders but couldn't because my friend looked as if he was in pain.

"Aaaahhhh," Anthony continued to yell. "Juan," he cried out to me raising his arms for me to lift him up from the chair. I ran over to him.

"Anthony, what's wrong?" I asked as his tears fell from his face as if he was in excruciating pain. The doctor backed away and walked toward the door.

"I'm gonna go get some tissues," she said as she walked out the room closing the door behind her. I grabbed Anthony and gave him a hug. I held him tight as he sobbed in my arms.

"Anthony, tell me what's wrong," I begged.

"I'm gonna die," he yelled as his cries got louder. The tears in my eyes started to swell.

"What do you mean you're gonna die? What's wrong"? I held on to Anthony as tightly as I could without him falling from the wheelchair.

"I got AIDS," he cried as he continued to hold me tight. I gathered him up and laid him down on the bed.

"Anthony, please calm down," I yelled with tears falling from my eyes. The doctor came back into the room with a box of tissues.

"Ahhh," continued Anthony as he grabbed the pillow and held it tight. I wiped my eyes with the back of my sleeve.

"Doctor, can you please tell me what's going on?" I asked. "I'm his next of kin," I added.

Anthony continued to yell as he bit into the pillow on the bed. The doctor reached for his chart that was on the bed.

"What's your name, sir?" she asked.

"Juan. Juan Jiles."

"Okay, sir, I see your name. Is he your brother?"

"Yes, my brother."

"Well, sir, your brother has AIDS."

"Oh, God," I yelled as the doctor grabbed me. My head was beginning to hurt. I felt weak. The next thing I knew, I was out cold on the floor.

XIV
No Negotiation

"This year's America's Next Top Model is...Tiffany," said Tyra Banks as I lay in the hospital bed snacking on some crackers that the nurse had brought me. My mother was asleep in the chair next to the table so I kept quiet because I didn't want to wake her.

At first, I didn't understand why I was in the hospital but the nurse told me that I'd had a nervous breakdown and I could go home today.

"Are you okay?" my mother asked as she squirmed from side to side in the chair. I could tell that it was uncomfortable by the look on her face.

"Oh, Mom, I'm sorry if the television was up too loud. I didn't mean to wake you," I said, still snacking on the crackers.

"It's okay, honey. I really couldn't sleep well in that chair," she said, getting up and walking over to me. She rested her hand on my arm.

"Baby, how are you really feeling?" she asked again.

I continued to chew the crackers before swallowing so I could speak. "Mom, I'm fine, really. Where's Anthony?" I asked, popping another cracker into my mouth.

My mother looked at me with tears in her eyes. She knew that Anthony and I had been friends for the longest. I stopped chewing the dry piece of cracker as I watched her reaction to my question. My tears fell instantly as my mother grabbed me and held me.

"Sweetheart, did you know that Anthony had AIDS?"

"Yes, Mommy, we just found out."

She came over to me and rubbed my face with her soft, delicate hands.

"Baby, Anthony's blood pressure was high and on top of the AIDS, we found out that he had type-2 diabetes."

My heart fell to my feet as I thought of my best friend lying in the hospital with tubes up his nose again. I couldn't stand it. I took a deep breath and looked my mom dead in the eyes.

"Is he gonna be okay?" I asked with a shaky voice.

My mother came over and grabbed me. The tears started running down my face. I didn't know what was going on. All I knew was that I wanted to see Anthony now. My mother held me tighter as she rocked me back and forth as we both cried.

"Sweetheart, Anthony is with God now. He didn't make it."

XV
PAYBACK'S A BITCH

On the day of Rob's funeral I was awakened to a hearty meal made by my one and only. I was grateful to have a man by my side at this time when it seemed as if all had failed.

Bryant came into the bedroom fully dressed in all black, waiting for me to dress so he could escort me to the funeral. He came and sat down on the side of the bed where I lay with my back against the headboard. He grabbed my hand as he lifted it to his mouth and kissed the back of my hand gently.

"I love you," he said exotically as if I didn't know.

"Bryant, I love you, too," I responded. He let my hand go and turned to face the window.

"You know, at this time, I really want to be honest with you," he said, looking down at the floor, then back at the window. "I'm a scared brother. You know I may walk around here acting all tough but, really, I'm scared. I have my whole life ahead of me and I'm scared. I want us to start going to church, you know?" He looked up at my face.

"I want to go to college and make something of myself. There's something else I want to be honest with you about." He turned to face me. "And I don't want you to love me any less because I did this."

"Bryant, what did you do?" I asked in anticipation. He took a deep breath and began to talk.

"I killed Melissa myself," he said without holding back. My heart raced. "I wanted to tell you that because in order for us to start out on the right foot, I thought you needed to know everything about me." He then turned to face the window.

At this time I became scared right along with him. I loved this man and was so sure that I wanted to spend the rest of my life with him.

"Baby, you're right. We need to know about each other's pasts. I've been wanting to tell you something about my dark past for a long time."

He turned around and looked me in my eyes. "What is it?" he asked with a serious look on his face.

I sighed as my eyes began tearing. "Before you and I started dating, I had a boyfriend named Darnell and he was very greedy for money. So he came up with a plan for us to rob a bank downtown and, at first, I wasn't with it but then..." Tears started to roll down my face. "Once my parents disowned me, I didn't have any money so he asked me to help him rob a bank and we would live comfortably together. So I did," I explained as I cried uncontrollably.

He looked at me with heated eyes, similar to the look he had when he was kicking my ass in his grandmother's basement. His eyes also began to swell with tears.

"Did anyone get hurt?" he asked firmly.

"I didn't mean for anyone to get hurt," I cried, now trembling and shaking at what he was about to do.

"I asked you a fuckin' question," he yelled with a tight fist. "Now, did anyone get hurt?" he asked again but this time he said it more calmly.

"Yes, Bryant. A few people got hurt."

"A few people, huh?" He stood up from the bed and turned around to face me. His eyes widened. "Who?"

"Bryant, I never knew their names. I didn't know those people," I explained.

"You didn't know those people but you know whether they were males or females," he yelled. He rushed over to me and gripped me by my neck. "You fuckin' faggot. Tell me who you hurt." He let my neck loose just enough so I could breath and tell him who had gotten hurt.

"Three people were shot. Two males and one female," I yelled as he knocked me across the bed with his fist. I yelled as I held my throbbing face and I began to cry all over again.

"That lady your boyfriend killed was my mother," he screamed from across the room as he came running toward me like a raging bull. Before he got the chance to get to me, two police officers came out of nowhere and pulled him away while my heart continued to beat rapidly.

"It's okay now, we got 'em," the Caucasian officer said, pulling Bryant away from me.

"You stay right there," he said, pointing to me. "Come on, Mr. Thompson, you did a great job," he added.

As the officer walked Bryant out of the room, three more officers came in; two white and one black.

"Hey, Mr. Jiles. I thought we would never get you to admit to the murders and the robbery, but now we have your confession on tape," said the white officer who held the cassette recorder that was once planted in Bryant's pocket.

"Get up slowly and put your hands behind your back, you fuckin' fag," said the black officer as he pulled his handcuffs out to cuff me.

$$$$$

Three months later
City Hall
Downtown, Philadelphia

"Please state your name for the court, please," said the African-American judge who sat on the bench during my trial.

"My name is Michelle Smith," stated the young lady whom I had seen before. I sat on the side of my attorney trying to figure out where I had seen her. The prosecuting attorney took his place on the floor. The bailiff swore her in before she sat down.

"Ms. Michelle, were you present at the bank during the robbery and the shooting of John McCants, Darnell Rhodes, and Beverly Vaughn?" he asked while walking in a circular motion.

"Yes, I was *working* in the bank at that time, sir," she answered in a sweet tone.

"Okay, Ms. Smith. Why aren't you working there now?" asked the prosecutor.

"Currently I am on maternity leave. I recently gave birth to a baby boy," she stated. I sat still in my seat as I revisited that day in my mind. *The bank, the gun, the girl—the girl was the pregnant teller. The girl—the teller—the same girl that hugged Bryant at his victory party. I was set the fuck up the entire time.*

I turned around to see Bryant, Loretta, and Ms. Bernice in the courtroom. She didn't look at me, not once, but Bryant kept his eyes on me the entire time.

"Can you point out the perpetrator in the courtroom, Ms. Smith?"

"Yes, I can."

"By all means, ma'am, please do so." She pointed her index finger straight at me.

"I thank you, Ms. Smith, you may step down. Your Honor, I would like to call my next witness for the drug-trafficking charges. She is currently being held at the Delaware County Prison for aggravated assault to her daughter but we brought her here today to testify against Mr. Jiles.

"The Commonwealth calls to the stand Ms. Melissa Childs, Your Honor." Two sheriffs brought Melissa from the chambers, sporting her county reds and then she took the stand.

"Please state your name for the courts, please."

"My name is Melissa Childs," she stated as she stared me up and down as if we were still on the streets and she wanted to fight me.

"Bailiff, swear her in, please," said the cocky prosecutor. Melissa raised her right hand.

"Do you swear to tell the truth and nothing but the truth so help you God?" said the bailiff who looked not a day over ninety.

"Yes," she lied.

"Okay, Ms. Childs, we're going to keep this thing simple. Did you actually see Juan Jiles take kilos of cocaine and other substances into his apartment?" the prosecutor asked.

"Yes," she lied again.

"Okay, Ms. Childs, is Juan Jiles in the courtroom today?"

"Yes."

"Can you point him out?"

"Yes, I can, he's sitting right there in the blue suit," she said.

"Okay, that will be all, Ms. Childs. I'm done," he said, walking over and taking his seat behind the desk. Melissa then got up and walked with the sheriffs out of the courtroom. I felt Bryant piercing the back of my head as I turned around.

The judge then gave Robert Datner the floor.

"Is there anything you would like to add before sentencing?" the judge asked before delivering his theme. Mr. Datner stood up next to me.

"My client is throwing himself at the mercy of the court, Your Honor," Mr. Datner said.

"Okay, would the defendant please rise?" I stood up and cupped my hands to the front of me, still turning around to get one last glance at Bryant as the judge began to speak.

"As the defendant throws himself at the mercy of the court, this court hereby sentences Juan Jiles to five to ten years in a state correctional facility for armed robbery and conspiracy to commit murder." The court gasped as Ms. Bernice started to sob. Bryant placed his arm around her as the judge banged his gavel.

"Quiet in this courtroom. I hereby sentence Juan Jiles to an additional five years in a correctional facility for drug trafficking along with a five-year stint for rehabilitation. That is all, thanks," said the judge before he banged his gavel again.

Mr. Datner had gotten me off good because I could've been spending more time for the murder of the security guard but Datner made it seem as if Darnell had shot at him first. Plus some of my time would be cut in half because I was using the drugs instead of selling them. *Thank you, Robert Datner.*

$$$$$

"Mail call," yelled the dark-skinned guy pushing the mail cart. "Here, you faggot. Someone wrote your stinking ass a letter." I looked at him and turned my nose up as I snatched the letter from his hand.

"Pussy," he said as I went back into my cell to read my letter. It didn't have a postmark where it came from so I opened it...

Dear J.J.

Lord knows I'm so sorry that you have to go through this. I want you to know that I'm not upset with you at all for what happened. I'm upset at the nigga who pulled the trigger on my mom. Like I said before you are the only nigga that I really dealt with like that and now that you're gone, it's makin' me sick. Baby, don't think I'm mad at you. I just wanted justice to be served, so my mother can rest in peace. Baby, I will always have your back. Trust me when I tell you, I'm gonna have a house, a car, and a life for you when you hit the streets. I will also take over the shop for you (don't worry.) Baby, you need to know that only you complete me. I miss your pretty ass so much. Always remember that I love you, Baby, and I'll always be grateful of you being In Love with this Thug.

Love, Bryant!

ABOUT THE AUTHOR

Reginald L. Hall is an *Essence* bestselling author and an outspoken advocate of gay rights. He has appeared on popular television talk shows, including *The Ricki Lake Show*, and is renowned for his controversial book *Memoir: Delaware County Prison*. He resides with his family outside Philadelphia. Visit his website www.reginaldsworld.com or www.myspace.com/reginaldsworld. You can email him at reginaldhall5413@aol.com

DRINKING TEA AND CHATTING ABOUT

In Love With a Thug

A story of an openly gay male who
falls into the arms of the wrong man.

In Love With a Thug, the new novel by the critically acclaimed, controversial author Reginald L. Hall takes you inside the world of an openly gay male, Juan Jiles.

Based in Philadelphia, Juan takes part in a bank robbery that leads to the death of his once thugged-out boyfriend, Darnell. After the mourning process is over, Juan takes the money earned from the robbery to open up one of Philly's most popular hair salons, where he meets and falls in love with sexy B-boy Bryant. Bryant has all the baggage that comes with dealing with a thug—the hustling, the lies, the beatings and, of course, the baby mama drama. Bryant introduces Juan to a world of drugs where he soon falls victim to the streets; causing him to lose his glamorous hair salon. Juan soon learns that the reason for Bryant's appearance is solely to tie up a few loose ends from his past.

Now that you've read the book, consider the following:

❐ Do you think Darnell was actually that much in love with Juan that he'd ask him to rob a bank and risk his life; or was Juan used?

❏ Do you think Juan made a smart decision with the money?

❏ Do you think Juan had enough time to mourn Darnell's death before he went out and splurged with the money?

❏ Instead of opening a hair salon, what's the best thing that Juan could have done with such a large amount of money?

❏ Was Juan's feelings lust or love for Bryant? Do you think Juan was looking for love but in all the wrong places or was his focus basically on thugs?

❏ Bryant could have done more to make Juan feel more wanted or needed. Was there ever a part where Juan felt as though Bryant was using him?

❏ Once Juan found out that Bryant was engaged to Mariah, should he have bailed then or taken Bryant's deception?

❏ Juan is considered to be a smart, level-headed person. Were all the decisions he made with the money the right ones?

❏ If not, more so than using drugs would you say he could have made more capital by selling drugs?

❏ With all the drama with Bryant's baby's mother and then the eye-drop incident, should Juan have opened his eyes and bailed? Or would it be wise to stand by your man and stick with whatever he's going through?

❐ Juan had a large sum of money in his bank account. Although he started using drugs do you think he still had the means and the will power to hold on to the shop?

❐ Do you think that Juan was Bryant's first gay lover?

❐ What do you think of Juan's relationship with his parents? Do you think either of his parents felt any remorse for disowning him? Do you think Juan truly forgave his father for abusing him?